The Go-Away Bird

KEYSTONE SHORT STORIES

THE GO-AWAY BIRD

and Other Stories

by

MURIEL SPARK

J. B. LIPPINCOTT COMPANY
Philadelphia   New York

To
DEREK STANFORD

Some of the stories in this book have appeared in the following publications: *The Norseman, Courier, Botteghe Oscure, The Observer, The Glasgow Herald, Punch,* and the late *World Review,* to which grateful acknowledgments are made.

CONTENTS

The Black Madonna

WHEN the Black Madonna was installed in the Church of the Sacred Heart the Bishop himself came to consecrate it. His long purple train was upheld by the two curliest of the choir. The day was favoured suddenly with thin October sunlight as he crossed the courtyard from the presbytery to the church, as the procession followed him chanting the Litany of the Saints: five priests in vestments of white heavy silk interwoven with glinting threads, four lay officials with straight red robes, then the confraternities and the tangled columns of the Mothers' Union.

The new town of Whitney Clay had a large proportion of Roman Catholics, especially among the nurses at the new hospital; and at the paper mills, too, there were many Catholics, drawn inland from Liverpool by the new housing estate; likewise, with the canning factories.

The Black Madonna had been given to the church by a recent convert. It was carved out of bog oak.

'They found the wood in the bog. Had been there hundreds of years. They sent for the sculptor right away by phone. He went over to Ireland and carved it there and then. You see, he had to do it while it was still wet.'

'Looks a bit like contemporary art.'

I

'Nah, that's not contemporary art, it's old-fashioned. If you'd ever seen contemporary work you'd *know* it was old-fashioned.'

'Looks like contemp——'

'It's old-*fashioned*. Else how'd it get sanctioned to be put up?'

'It's not so nice as the Immaculate Conception at Lourdes. That lifts you up.'

Everyone got used, eventually, to the Black Madonna with her square hands and straight carved draperies. There was a movement to dress it up in vestments, or at least a lace veil.

'She looks a bit gloomy, Father, don't you think?'

'No,' said the priest, 'I think it looks fine. If you start dressing it up in cloth you'll spoil the line.'

Sometimes people came from London especially to see the Black Madonna, and these were not Catholics; they were, said the priest, probably no religion at all, poor souls, though gifted with faculties. They came, as if to a museum, to see the line of the Black Madonna which must not be spoiled by vestments.

The new town of Whitney Clay had swallowed up the old village. One or two cottages with double dormer windows, an inn called 'The Tyger', a Methodist chapel and three small shops represented the village; the three shops were already threatened by the Council; the Methodists were fighting to keep their chapel. Only the double dormer cottages and the inn were protected by the Nation and so had to be suffered by the Town Planning Committee.

The town was laid out like geometry in squares, arcs (to allow for the by-pass) and isosceles triangles, breaking off, at one point, to skirt the old village which, from the aerial view, looked like a merry doodle on the page.

Manders Road was one side of a parallelogram of green-bordered streets. It was named after one of the founders of the canning concern, Manders' Figs in Syrup, and it comprised a row of shops and a long high block of flats named Cripps House after the late Sir Stafford Cripps who had laid the foundation stone. In flat twenty-two on the fifth floor of Cripps House lived Raymond and Lou Parker. Raymond Parker was a foreman at the motor works, and was on the management committee. He had been married for fifteen years to Lou, who was thirty-seven at the time that the miraculous powers of the Black Madonna came to be talked of.

Of the twenty-five couples who live in Cripps House five were Catholics. All, except Raymond and Lou Parker, had children. A sixth family had recently been moved by the Council into one of the six-roomed houses because of the seven children besides the grandfather.

Raymond and Lou were counted lucky to have obtained their three-roomed flat although they had no children. People with children had priority; but their name had been on the waiting list for years, and some said Raymond had a pull with one of the Councillors who was a director of the motor works.

The Parkers were among the few tenants of Cripps House who owned a motor car. They did not, like most of their neighbours, have a television receiver, for being childless they had been able to afford to expand themselves in the way of taste, so that their habits differed slightly and their amusements considerably, from those of their neighbours. The Parkers went to the pictures only when *The Observer* had praised the film; they considered television not their sort of thing; they adhered to their religion; they voted Labour; they believed that the twentieth century was the best so far; they assented to the doctrine of original sin; they frequently applied the word 'Victorian' to ideas and people they did not like — for instance, when a local Town Councillor resigned his office Raymond said, 'He had to go. He's Victorian. And far too young for the job'; and Lou said Jane Austen's books were too Victorian; and anyone who opposed the abolition of capital punishment was Victorian. Raymond took the *Reader's Digest*, a magazine called *Motoring* and *The Catholic Herald*. Lou took *The Queen, Woman's Own* and *Life*. Their daily paper was *The News Chronicle*. They read two books apiece each week. Raymond preferred travel books; Lou liked novels.

For the first five years of their married life they had been worried about not having children. Both had submitted themselves to medical tests as a result of which Lou had a course of injections. These were unsuccessful. It had been a special disappointment since both came from large sprawling Catholic families. None of their married brothers and sisters had less than three children. One of Lou's sisters, now widowed, had eight; they sent her a pound a week.

Their flat in Cripps House had three rooms and a kitchen. All round them their neighbours were saving up to buy houses. A council flat, once obtained, was a mere platform in space to further the progress of the rocket. This ambition was not shared by Raymond

4

and Lou; they were not only content, they were delighted, with these civic chambers, and indeed took something of an aristocratic view of them, not without a self-conscious feeling of being free, in this particular, from the prejudices of that middle class to which they as good as belonged. 'One day,' said Lou, 'it will be the thing to live in a council flat.'

They were eclectic as to their friends. Here, it is true, they differed slightly from each other. Raymond was for inviting the Ackleys to meet the Farrells. Mr. Ackley was an accountant at the Electricity Board. Mr. and Mrs. Farrell were respectively a sorter at Manders' Figs in Syrup and an usherette at the Odeon.

'After all,' argued Raymond, 'they're all Catholics.'

'Ah well,' said Lou, 'but now, their interests are different. The Farrells wouldn't know what the Ackleys were talking about. The Ackleys like politics. The Farrells like to tell jokes. I'm not a snob, only sensible.'

'Oh, please yourself.' For no-one could call Lou a snob, and everyone knew she was sensible.

Their choice of acquaintance was wide by reason of their active church membership: that is to say, they were members of various guilds and confraternities. Raymond was a sidesman, and he also organised the weekly football lottery in aid of the Church Decoration Fund. Lou felt rather out of things when the Mothers' Union met and had special Masses, for the Mothers' Union was the only group she did not qualify for. Having been a nurse before her marriage she was, however, a member of the Nurses' Guild.

Thus, most of their Catholic friends came from different departments of life. Others, connected with

5

the motor works where Raymond was a foreman,
were of different social grades to which Lou was
more alive than Raymond. He let her have her way,
as a rule, when it came to a question of which would
mix with which.

A dozen Jamaicans were taken on at the motor works.
Two came into Raymond's department. He invited
them to the flat one evening to have coffee. They were
unmarried, very polite and black. The quiet one was
called Henry Pierce and the talkative one, Oxford
St. John. Lou, to Raymond's surprise and pleasure,
decided that all their acquaintance, from top to bottom,
must meet Henry and Oxford. All along he had known
she was not a snob, only sensible, but he had rather
feared she would consider the mixing of their new
black and their old white friends not sensible.

'I'm glad you like Henry and Oxford,' he said.
'I'm glad we're able to introduce them to so many
people.' For the dark pair had, within a month, spent
nine evenings at Cripps House; they had met account-
ants, teachers, packers and sorters. Only Tina Farrell,
the usherette, had not seemed to understand the quality
of these occasions: 'Quite nice chaps, them darkies,
when you get to know them.'

'You mean Jamaicans,' said Lou. 'Why shouldn't
they be nice? They're no different from anyone else.'

'Yes, yes, that's what I mean,' said Tina.

'We're all equal,' stated Lou. 'Don't forget there
are black Bishops.'

'Jesus, I never said we were the equal of a Bishop,'
Tina said, very bewildered.

'Well, don't call them darkies.'

Sometimes, on summer Sunday afternoons Raymond

and Lou took their friends for a run in their car, ending up at a riverside road-house. The first time they turned up with Oxford and Henry they felt defiant; but there were no objections, there was no trouble at all. Soon the dark pair ceased to be a novelty. Oxford St. John took up with a pretty red-haired bookkeeper, and Henry Pierce, missing his companion, spent more of his time at the Parkers' flat. Lou and Raymond had planned to spend their two weeks' summer holiday in London. 'Poor Henry,' said Lou. 'He'll miss us.'

Once you brought him out he was not so quiet as you thought at first. Henry was twenty-four, desirous of knowledge in all fields, shining very much in eyes, skin, teeth, which made him seem all the more eager. He called out the maternal in Lou, and to some extent the avuncular in Raymond. Lou used to love him when he read out lines from his favourite poems which he had copied into an exercise book.

> *Haste thee, nymph, and bring with thee*
> *Jest and youthful jollity,*
> *Sport that . . .*

Lou would interrupt: 'You should say jest, jollity — not yest, yollity.'

'Jest,' he said carefully. 'And laughter holding both his sides,' he continued. '*Laughter* — hear that, Lou? — *laughter*. That's what the human race was made for. Those folks that go round gloomy, Lou, they . . .'

Lou loved this talk. Raymond puffed his pipe benignly. After Henry had gone Raymond would say what a pity it was such an intelligent young fellow had lapsed. For Henry had been brought up in a Roman

7

Catholic mission. He had, however, abandoned religion. He was fond of saying, 'The superstition of to-day is the science of yesterday.'

'I can't allow,' Raymond would say, 'that the Catholic Faith is superstition. I can't allow that.'

'He'll return to the Church one day' — this was Lou's contribution, whether Henry was present or not. If she said it in front of Henry he would give her an angry look. These were the only occasions when Henry lost his cheerfulness and grew quiet again.

Raymond and Lou prayed for Henry, that he might regain his faith. Lou said her rosary three times a week before the Black Madonna.

'He'll miss us when we go on our holidays.'

Raymond telephoned to the hotel in London. 'Have you a single room for a young gentleman accompanying Mr. and Mrs. Parker?' He added, 'a coloured gentleman.' To his pleasure a room was available, and to his relief there was no objection to Henry's colour.

They enjoyed their London holiday, but it was somewhat marred by a visit to that widowed sister of Lou's to whom she allowed a pound a week towards the rearing of her eight children. Lou had not seen her sister Elizabeth for nine years.

They went to her one day towards the end of their holiday. Henry sat at the back of the car beside a large suitcase stuffed with old clothes for Elizabeth. Raymond at the wheel kept saying, 'Poor Elizabeth — eight kids,' which irritated Lou, though she kept her peace.

Outside the underground station at Victoria Park, where they stopped to ask the way, Lou felt a strange sense of panic. Elizabeth lived in a very downward quarter of Bethnal Green, and in the past nine years since she had seen her Lou's memory of the shabby ground-floor rooms with their peeling walls and bare boards, had made a kinder nest for itself. Sending off the postal order to her sister each week she had gradually come to picture the habitation at Bethnal Green in an almost monastic light; it would be bare but well-scrubbed, spotless, and shining with Brasso and holy poverty. The floor boards gleamed. Elizabeth was grey-haired, lined, but neat. The children well behaved, sitting down betimes to their broth in two rows along an almost refectory table. It was not till they had reached Victoria Park that Lou felt the full force of the fact that everything would be different from what she had imagined. 'It may have gone down since I was last there,' she said to Raymond who had never visited Elizabeth before.

'What's gone down?'

'Poor Elizabeth's place.'

Lou had not taken much notice of Elizabeth's dull little monthly letters, almost illiterate, for Elizabeth, as she herself always said, was not much of a scholar. 'James is at another job I hope thats the finish of the bother I had my blood presiure there was a Health visitor very nice. Also the assistance they sent my Dinner all the time and for the kids at home they call it meals on Wheels. I pray to the Almighty that James is well out of his bother he never lets on at sixteen their all the same never open his mouth but Gods eyes are not shut. Thanks for P.O. you will be rewarded your affect sister Elizabeth.'

Lou tried to piece together in her mind the gist of

9

nine years' such letters. James was the eldest; she
supposed he had been in trouble.

'I ought to have asked Elizabeth about young
James,' said Lou. 'She wrote to me last year that he
was in a bother, there was talk of him being sent away,
but I didn't take it in at the time, I was busy.'

'You can't take everything on your shoulders,'
said Raymond. 'You do very well by Elizabeth.'
They had pulled up outside the house where Elizabeth
lived on the ground floor. Lou looked at the chipped
paint, the dirty windows and torn grey-white curtains
and was reminded with startling clarity of her hopeless childhood in Liverpool from which, miraculously,
hope had lifted her, and had come true, for the nuns
had got her that job; and she had trained as a nurse
among white-painted beds, and white shining walls,
and tiles, hot water everywhere and Dettol without
stint. When she had first married she had wanted all
white-painted furniture that you could wash and
liberate from germs; but Raymond had been for oak,
he did not understand the pleasure of hygiene and
new enamel paint, for his upbringing had been orderly,
he had been accustomed to a lounge suite and autumn
tints in the front room all his life. And now Lou stood
and looked at the outside of Elizabeth's place and
felt she had gone right back.

On the way back to the hotel Lou chattered with
relief that it was over. 'Poor Elizabeth, she hasn't had
much of a chance. I liked little Francis, what did you
think of little Francis, Ray?'

Raymond did not like being called Ray, but he made
no objection for he knew that Lou had been under a

strain. Elizabeth had not been very pleasant. She had expressed admiration for Lou's hat, bag, gloves and shoes which were all navy blue, but she had used an accusing tone. The house had been smelly and dirty. 'I'll show you round,' Elizabeth had said in a tone of mock refinement, and they were forced to push through a dark narrow passage behind her skinny form till they came to the big room where the children slept. A row of old iron beds each with a tumble of dark blanket rugs, no sheets. Raymond was indignant at the sight and hoped that Lou was not feeling upset. He knew very well Elizabeth had a decent living income from a number of public sources, and was simply a slut, one of those who would not help themselves.

'Ever thought of taking a job, Elizabeth?' he had said, and immediately realised his stupidity. But Elizabeth took her advantage. 'What d'you mean? *I'm* not going to leave my kids in no nursery. *I'm* not going to send them to no home. What kids need these days is a good home life and that's what they get.' And she added, 'God's eyes are not shut,' in a tone which was meant for him, Raymond, to get at him for doing well in life.

Raymond distributed half-crowns to the younger children and deposited on the table half-crowns for those who were out playing in the street.

'Goin' already?' said Elizabeth in her tone of reproach. But she kept eyeing Henry with interest, and the reproachful tone was more or less a routine affair.

'You from the States?' Elizabeth said to Henry.

Henry sat on the edge of his sticky chair and answered, no, from Jamaica, while Raymond winked at him to cheer him.

'During the war there was a lot of boys like you from the States,' Elizabeth said, giving him a sideways look.

Henry held out his hand to the second youngest child, a girl of seven, and said, 'Come talk to me.'

The child said nothing, only dipped into the box of sweets which Lou had brought.

'Come talk,' said Henry.

Elizabeth laughed. 'If she does talk you'll be sorry you ever asked. She's got a tongue in her head, that one. You should hear her cheeking up to the teachers.' Elizabeth's bones jerked with laughter among her loose clothes. There was a lopsided double bed in the corner, and beside it a table cluttered with mugs, tins, a comb and brush, a number of hair curlers, a framed photograph of the Sacred Heart, and also Raymond noticed what he thought erroneously to be a box of contraceptives. He decided to say nothing to Lou about this; he was quite sure she must have observed other things which he had not; possibly things of a more distressing nature.

Lou's chatter on the way back to the hotel had a touch of hysteria. 'Raymond, dear,' she said in her most chirpy west-end voice, 'I simply *had* to give the poor dear *all* my next week's housekeeping money. We shall have to starve, darling, when we get home. That's *simply* what we shall have to do.'

'O.K.,' said Raymond.

'I ask you,' Lou shrieked, 'what else could I do, what *could* I do?'

'Nothing at all,' said Raymond, 'but what you've done.'

'My own *sister*, my dear,' said Lou; 'and did you

see the way she had her hair bleached? — All streaky, and she used to have a lovely head of hair.'

'I wonder if she tries to raise herself?' said Raymond. 'With all those children she could surely get better accommodation if only she——'

'That sort,' said Henry, leaning forward from the back of the car, 'never moves. It's the slum mentality, man. Take some folks I've seen back home——'

'There's no comparison,' Lou snapped suddenly, 'this is quite a different case.'

Raymond glanced at her in surprise; Henry sat back, offended. Lou was thinking wildly, what a cheek *him* talking like a snob. At least Elizabeth's white.

Their prayers for the return of faith to Henry Pierce were so far answered in that he took a tubercular turn which was followed by a religious one. He was sent off to a sanatorium in Wales with a promise from Lou and Raymond to visit him before Christmas. Meantime, they applied themselves to Our Lady for the restoration of Henry's health.

Oxford St. John, whose love affair with the red-haired girl had come to grief, now frequented their flat, but he could never quite replace Henry in their affections. Oxford was older and less refined than Henry. He would stand in front of the glass in their kitchen and tell himself, 'Man, you just a big black bugger.' He kept referring to himself as black, which of course he was, Lou thought, but it was not the thing to say. He stood in the doorway with his arms and smile thrown wide: 'I am black but comely, O ye daughters of Jerusalem.' And once, when Raymond was out, Oxford brought the conversation round to that question of being black *all over*, which made Lou very uncomfortable and she kept looking at the clock and dropped stitches in her knitting.

Three times a week when she went to the black Our Lady with her rosary to ask for the health of Henry Pierce, she asked also that Oxford St. John would get another job in another town, for she did not like to make objections, telling her feelings to Raymond; there were no objections to make that you could put your finger on. She could not very well complain that Oxford was common; Raymond despised snobbery, and so did she, it was a very delicate question. She was amazed when, within three weeks, Oxford announced that he was thinking of looking for a job in Manchester.

Lou said to Raymond, 'Do you know, there's something *in* what they say about the bog oak statue in the church.'

'There may be,' said Raymond. 'People say so.'

Lou could not tell him how she had petitioned the removal of Oxford St. John. But when she got a letter from Henry Pierce to say he was improving, she told Raymond, 'You see, we asked for Henry to get back the Faith, and so he did. Now we ask for his recovery and he's improving.'

'He's having good treatment at the sanatorium,' Raymond said. But he added, 'Of course we'll have to keep up the prayers.' He himself, though not a rosary man, knelt before the Black Madonna every Saturday evening after Benediction to pray for Henry Pierce.

Whenever they saw Oxford he was talking of leaving Whitney Clay. Raymond said, 'He's making a big

14

mistake going to Manchester. A big place can be very lonely. I hope he'll change his mind.'

'He won't,' said Lou, so impressed was she now by the powers of the Black Madonna. She was good and tired of Oxford St. John with his feet up on her cushions, and calling himself a nigger.

'We'll miss him,' said Raymond, 'he's such a cheery big soul.'

'We will,' said Lou. She was reading the parish magazine, which she seldom did, although she was one of the voluntary workers who sent them out, addressing hundreds of wrappers every month. She had vaguely noticed, in previous numbers, various references to the Black Madonna, how she had granted this or that favour. Lou had heard that people sometimes came from neighbouring parishes to pray at the Church of the Sacred Heart because of the statue. Some said they came from all over England, but whether this was to admire the art-work or to pray, Lou was not sure. She gave her attention to the article in the parish magazine:

While not wishing to make excessive claims . . . many prayers answered and requests granted to the Faithful in an exceptional way . . . two remarkable cures effected, but medical evidence is, of course, still in reserve, a certain lapse of time being necessary to ascertain permanency of cure. The first of these cases was a child of twelve suffering from leukaemia. . . . The second . . . While not desiring to create a *cultus* where none is due, we must remember it is always our duty to honour Our Blessed Lady, the dispenser of all graces, to whom we owe . . .

15

Another aspect of the information received by the Father Rector concerning our 'Black Madonna' is one pertaining to childless couples of which three cases have come to his notice. In each case the couple claim to have offered constant devotion to the 'Black Madonna,' and in two of the cases specific requests were made for the favour of a child. In *all* cases the prayers were answered. The proud parents. . . . It should be the loving duty of every parishioner to make a special thanksgiving. . . . The Father Rector will be grateful for any further information. . . .

'Look, Raymond,' said Lou. 'Read this.'

They decided to put in for a baby to the Black Madonna.

The following Saturday, when they drove to the church for Benediction Lou jangled her rosary. Raymond pulled up outside the church. 'Look here, Lou,' he said, 'do you want a baby in any case?' — for he partly thought she was only putting the Black Madonna to the test — 'Do you want a child, after all these years?'

This was a new thought to Lou. She considered her neat flat and tidy routine, the entertaining with her good coffee cups, the weekly papers and the library books, the tastes which they would not have been able to cultivate had they had a family of children. She thought of her nice young looks which everyone envied, and her freedom of movement.

'Perhaps we should try,' she said. 'God won't give us a child if we aren't meant to have one.'

'We have to make some decisions for ourselves,' he

said. 'And to tell you the truth if *you* don't want a child, *I* don't.'

'There's no harm in praying for one,' she said.

'You have to be careful what you pray for,' he said. 'You mustn't tempt Providence.'

She thought of her relatives, and Raymond's, all married with children. She thought of her sister Elizabeth with her eight, and remembered that one who cheeked up to the teachers, so pretty and sulky and shabby, and she remembered the fat baby Francis sucking his dummy and clutching Elizabeth's bony neck.

'I don't see why I shouldn't have a baby,' said Lou.

Oxford St. John departed at the end of the month. He promised to write, but they were not surprised when weeks passed and they had no word. 'I don't suppose we shall ever hear from him again,' said Lou. Raymond thought he detected satisfaction in her voice, and would have thought she was getting snobbish as women do as they get older, losing sight of their ideals, had she not gone on to speak of Henry Pierce. Henry had written to say he was nearly cured, but had been advised to return to the West Indies.

'We must go and see him,' said Lou. 'We promised. What about the Sunday after next?'

'O.K.,' said Raymond.

It was the Saturday before that Sunday when Lou had her first sick turn. She struggled out of bed to attend Benediction, but had to leave suddenly during the service and was sick behind the church in the presbytery yard. Raymond took her home, though she protested against cutting out her rosary to the Black Madonna.

'After only six weeks!' she said, and she could hardly tell whether her sickness was due to excitement or nature. 'Only six weeks ago,' she said — and her voice had a touch of its old Liverpool — 'did we go to that Black Madonna and the prayer's answered, see.'

Raymond looked at her in awe as he held the bowl for her sickness. 'Are you sure?' he said.

She was well enough next day to go to visit Henry in the sanatorium. He was fatter and, she thought, a little coarser: and tough in his manner, as if once having been nearly disembodied he was not going to let it happen again. He was leaving the country very soon. He promised to come and see them before he left. Lou barely skimmed through his next letter before handing it over to Raymond.

Their visitors, now, were ordinary white ones. 'Not so colourful,' Raymond said, 'as Henry and Oxford were.' Then he looked embarrassed lest he should seem to be making a joke about the word coloured.

'Do you miss the niggers?' said Tina Farrell, and Lou forgot to correct her.

Lou gave up most of her church work in order to sew and knit for the baby. Raymond gave up the *Reader's Digest*. He applied for promotion and got it; he became a departmental manager. The flat was now a waiting-room for next summer, after the baby was born, when they would put down the money for a house. They hoped for one of the new houses on a building site on the outskirts of the town.

'We shall need a garden,' Lou explained to her friends. 'I'll join the Mothers' Union,' she thought.

Meantime the spare bedroom was turned into a nursery. Raymond made a cot, regardless that some of the neighbours complained of the hammering. Lou prepared a cradle, trimmed it with frills. She wrote to her relatives; she wrote to Elizabeth, sent her five pounds, and gave notice that there would be no further weekly payments, seeing that they would now need every penny.

'She doesn't require it, anyway,' said Raymond. 'The Welfare State looks after people like Elizabeth.' And he told Lou about the contraceptives he thought he had seen on the table by the double bed. Lou became very excited about this. 'How did you know they were contraceptives? What did they look like? Why didn't you tell me before? What a cheek, calling herself a Catholic, do you think she has a man, then?'

Raymond was sorry he had mentioned the subject.

'Don't worry, dear, don't upset yourself, dear.'

'And she told me she goes to Mass every Sunday, and all the kids go excepting James. No wonder he's got into trouble with an example like that. I might have known, with her peroxide hair. A pound a week I've been sending up to now, that's fifty-two pounds a year. I would never have done it, calling herself a Catholic with birth control by her bedside.'

'Don't upset yourself, dear.'

Lou prayed to the Black Madonna three times a week for a safe delivery and a healthy child. She gave her story to the Father Rector who announced it in the next parish magazine. 'Another case has come to light of the kindly favour of our "Black Madonna" towards a childless couple . . .' Lou recited her rosary before the statue until it was difficult for her to kneel, and, when she stood, could not see her feet. The Mother of God with her black bog-oaken drapery, her high black cheekbones and square hands looked more virginal than ever to Lou as she stood counting her beads in front of her stomach.

She said to Raymond, 'If it's a girl we must have Mary as one of the names. But not the first name, it's too ordinary.'

'Please yourself, dear,' said Raymond. The doctor had told him it might be a difficult birth.

'Thomas, if it's a boy,' she said, 'after my uncle. But if it's a girl I'd like something fancy for a first name.'

He thought, Lou's slipping, she didn't used to say that word, fancy.

'What about Dawn?' she said. 'I like the sound of Dawn. Then Mary for a second name. Dawn Mary Parker, it sounds sweet.'

'Dawn! That's not a Christian name,' he said. Then he told her, 'Just as you please, dear.'

'Or Thomas Parker,' she said.

She had decided to go into the maternity wing of the hospital like everyone else. But near the time she let Raymond change her mind, since he kept saying, 'At your age, dear, it might be more difficult than for the younger women. Better book a private ward, we'll manage the expense.'

In fact, it was a very easy birth, a girl. Raymond was allowed in to see Lou in the late afternoon. She was half asleep. 'The nurse will take you to see the baby in the nursery ward,' she told him. 'She's lovely, but terribly red.'

'They're always red at birth,' said Raymond.

He met the nurse in the corridor. 'Any chance of seeing the baby? My wife said . . .'

She looked flustered. 'I'll get the Sister,' she said.

'Oh, I don't want to give any trouble, only my wife said——'

'That's all right. Wait here, Mr. Parker.'

The Sister appeared, a tall grave woman. Raymond thought her to be short-sighted for she seemed to look at him fairly closely before she bade him follow her.

The baby was round and very red, with dark curly hair.

'Fancy her having hair. I thought they were born bald,' said Raymond.

'They sometimes have hair at birth,' said the Sister.

'She's very red in colour.' Raymond began comparing his child with those in the other cots. 'Far more so than the others.'

'Oh, that will wear off.'

Next day he found Lou in a half-stupor. She had been given a strong sedative following an attack of screaming hysteria. He sat by her bed, bewildered. Presently a nurse beckoned him from the door. 'Will you have a word with Matron?'

'Your wife is upset about her baby,' said the matron. 'You see, the colour. She's a beautiful baby, perfect. It's a question of the colour.'

'I noticed the baby was red,' said Raymond, 'but the nurse said——'

'Oh, the red will go. It changes, you know. But the baby will certainly be brown, if not indeed black, as indeed we think she will be. A beautiful healthy child.'

'Black?' said Raymond.

'Yes, indeed we think so, indeed I must say, certainly so,' said the matron. 'We did not expect your wife to take it so badly when we told her. We've had plenty of dark babies here, but most of the mothers expect it.'

'There must be a mix-up. You must have mixed up the babies,' said Raymond.

'There's no question of mix-up,' said the matron sharply. 'We'll soon settle that. We've had some of *that* before.'

'But neither of us are dark,' said Raymond. 'You've seen my wife. You see me——'

'That's something you must work out for yourselves. I'd have a word with the doctor if I were you. But whatever conclusion you come to, please don't upset your wife at this stage. She has already refused to feed the child, says it isn't hers, which is ridiculous.'

'Was it Oxford St. John?' said Raymond.

'Raymond, the doctor told you not to come here upsetting me. I'm feeling terrible.'

'Was it Oxford St. John?'

'Clear out of here, you swine, saying things like that.'

He demanded to be taken to see the baby, as he had done every day for a week. The nurses were gathered round it, neglecting the squalling whites in the other cots for the sight of their darling black. She was indeed quite black, with a woolly crop and tiny negroid nostrils. She had been baptised that morning, though not in her parents' presence. One of the nurses had stood as godmother.

22

The nurses dispersed in a flurry as Raymond approached. He looked hard at the baby. It looked back with its black button eyes. He saw the name-tab round its neck, 'Dawn Mary Parker.'

He got hold of a nurse in the corridor. 'Look here, you just take that name Parker off that child's neck. The name's not Parker, it isn't my child.'

The nurse said, 'Get away, we're busy.'

'There's just a *chance*,' said the doctor to Raymond, 'that if there's ever been black blood in your family or your wife's, it's coming out now. It's a very long chance. I've never known it happen in my experience, but I've heard of cases, I could read them up.'

'There's nothing like that in my family,' said Raymond. He thought of Lou, the obscure Liverpool antecedents. The parents had died before he had met Lou.

'It could be several generations back,' said the doctor.

Raymond went home, avoiding the neighbours who would stop him to enquire after Lou. He rather regretted smashing up the cot in his first fury. That was something low coming out in him. But again, when he thought of the tiny black hands of the baby with their pink fingernails he did not regret smashing the cot.

He was successful in tracing the whereabouts of Oxford St. John. Even before he heard the result of Oxford's blood test he said to Lou, 'Write and ask your relations if there's been any black blood in the family.'

'Write and ask *yours*,' she said.

She refused to look at the black baby. The nurses

fussed round it all day, and came to report its progress to Lou.

'Pull yourself together, Mrs. Parker, she's a lovely child.'

'You must care for your infant,' said the priest.

'You don't know what I'm suffering,' Lou said.

'In the name of God,' said the priest, 'if you're a Catholic Christian you've got to expect to suffer.'

'I can't go against my nature,' said Lou. 'I can't be expected to——'

Raymond said to her one day in the following week, 'The blood tests are all right, the doctor says.'

'What do you mean, all right?'

'Oxford's blood and the baby's don't tally, and——'

'Oh, shut up,' she said. 'The baby's black and your blood tests can't make it white.'

'No,' he said. He had fallen out with his mother, through his enquiries whether there had been coloured blood in his family. 'The doctor says,' he said, 'that these black mixtures sometimes occur in seaport towns. It might have been generations back.'

'One thing,' said Lou. 'I'm not going to take that child back to the flat.'

'You'll have to,' he said.

Elizabeth wrote her a letter which Raymond intercepted:

'Dear Lou Raymond is asking if we have any blacks in the family well thats funny you have a coloured God is not asleep. There was that Flinn cousin Tommy at Liverpool he was very dark they put it down to the past a nigro off a ship that would be before our late Mothers Time God rest her soul she would turn in her grave you shoud have kept up your bit to me whats a pound a Week to you. It was on our fathers side the colour and Mary Flinn you remember at the dairy was dark remember her hare was like nigro hare it must be back in the olden days the nigro some ansester but it is only nature. I thank the almighty it has missed my kids and your hubby must think it was that nigro you was showing off when you came to my place. I wish you all the best as a widow with kids you shoud send my money as per usual your affec sister Elizabeth.'

'I gather from Elizabeth,' said Raymond to Lou, 'that there *was* some element of colour in your family. Of course, you couldn't be expected to know about it. I do think, though, that some kind of record should be kept.'

'Oh, shut *up*,' said Lou. 'The baby's black and nothing can make it white.'

Two days before Lou left the hospital she had a visitor, although she had given instructions that no-one except Raymond should be let in to see her. This lapse she attributed to the nasty curiosity of the nurses, for it was Henry Pierce come to say goodbye before embarkation. He stayed less than five minutes.

'Why, Mrs. Parker, your visitor didn't stay long,' said the nurse.

'No, I soon got rid of him. I thought I made it clear to you that I didn't want to see anyone. You shouldn't have let him in.'

'Oh, sorry, Mrs. Parker, but the young gentleman looked so upset when we told him so. He said he was going abroad and it was his last chance, he might never see you again. He said, "How's the baby?" and we said, "Tip-top."'

'I know what's in your mind,' said Lou. 'But it isn't true. I've got the blood tests.'

'Oh, Mrs. Parker, I wouldn't suggest for a minute...'

'She must have went with one of they niggers that used to come.'

Lou could never be sure if that was what she heard from the doorways and landings as she climbed the stairs of Cripps House, the neighbours hushing their conversation as she approached.

'I can't take to the child. Try as I do, I simply can't even like it.'

'Nor me,' said Raymond. 'Mind you, if it was anyone else's child I would think it was all right. It's just the thought of it being mine, and people thinking it isn't.'

'That's just it,' she said.

One of Raymond's colleagues had asked him that day how his friends Oxford and Henry were getting on. Raymond had to look twice before he decided that the question was innocent. But one never knew. . . . Already Lou and Raymond had approached the adoption society. It was now only a matter of waiting for word.

'If that child was mine,' said Tina Farrell, 'I'd never part with her. I wish we could afford to adopt another. She's the loveliest little darkie in the world.'

'You wouldn't think so,' said Lou, 'if she really was yours. Imagine it for yourself, waking up to find you've had a black baby that everyone thinks has a nigger for its father.'

'It *would* be a shock,' Tina said, and tittered.

'We've got the blood tests,' said Lou quickly.

Raymond got a transfer to London. They got word about the adoption very soon.

'We've done the right thing,' said Lou. 'Even the priest had to agree with that, considering how strongly we felt against keeping the child.'

'Oh, he said it was a good thing?'

'No, not a *good* thing. In fact he said it would have been a good thing if we could have kept the baby. But failing that, we did the *right* thing. Apparently, there's a difference.'

The Pawnbroker's Wife

AT Sea Point, on the coast of the Cape of Good Hope, in 1942, there was everywhere the sight of rejoicing, there was the sound of hilarity, and the sea washed up each day one or two bodies of servicemen in all kinds of uniform. The waters round the Cape were heavily mined. The people flocked to bring in the survivors. The girls of the seashore and harbour waited two by two for the troops on shore-leave from ships which had managed to enter the bay safely.

I was waiting for a ship to take me to England, and lived on the sea front in the house of Mrs. Jan Cloote, a pawnbroker's wife. From her window where, in the cool evenings, she sat knitting khaki socks till her eyes ached, Mrs. Jan Cloote took note of these happenings, and whenever I came in or went out she would open her door a little, and, standing in the narrow aperture, would tell me the latest.

She was a small woman of about forty-three, a native of Somerset. Her husband, Jan Cloote, had long ago disappeared into the Transvaal, where he was living, it was understood, with a native woman. With his wife, he had left three daughters, the house on the sea front, and, at the back of the house which opened on to a little mean street, a pawnshop.

Mrs. Jan Cloote had more or less built up everything that her husband had left half-finished. The house was in better repair than it ever had been, and she let off most of the rooms. The pawnshop had so far flourished that Mrs. Jan Cloote was able to take a shop next door where she sold a second-hand miscellany, unredeemed from the pawnshop. The three daughters had likewise flourished. From all accounts, they had gone barefoot to school at the time of their father's residence at home, because all his profit had gone on his two opulent passions, yellow advocaat and black girls. As I saw the daughters now, I could hardly credit their unfortunate past life. The youngest, Isa, was a schoolgirl with long yellow plaits, and she was quite a voluptuary in her manner. The other two, in their late teens, were more like the mother, small, shy, quiet, lady-like, secretarial and discreet. Greta and Maida, they were called.

It was seldom that Mrs. Jan Cloote opened the door of her own apartment wide enough for anyone to see inside. This was a habit of the whole family, but they had nothing really to hide, that one could see. And there Mrs. Jan Cloote would stand, with one of the girls, perhaps, looking over her shoulder, wedged in the narrow doorway, and the door not twelve inches open. The hall was very dark, and being a frugal woman, she did not keep a bulb in the hall light, which therefore did not function.

One day, as I came in, I saw her little shape, the thin profile and knobbly bun, outlined against the light within her rooms.

'Sh-sh-sh,' she said.

'Can you come in tonight for a *little* cup of tea with

29

the others?' she said in a hushed breath. And I understood, as I accepted, that the need for the hush had something to do with the modesty of the proposed party, conveyed in the words, 'a *little* cup . . .'

I knocked on her door after dinner. Maida opened it just wide enough for me to enter, then closed it again quickly. Some of the other lodgers were there: a young man who worked in an office on the docks, and a retired insurance agent and his wife.

Isa, the schoolgirl, arrived presently. I was surprised to see that she was heavily made up on the mouth and eyes.

'Another troopship gone down,' stated Isa.

'Hush, dear,' said her mother; 'we are not supposed to talk about the shipping.'

Mrs. Jan Cloote winked at me as she said this. It struck me then that she was very proud of Isa.

'An Argentine boat in,' said Isa.

'Really?' said Mrs. Jan Cloote. 'Any nice chaps?'

The old couple looked at each other. The young man, who was new to many things, looked puzzled but said nothing. Maida and Greta, like their mother, seemed agog for news.

'A lot of nice ones, eh?' said Maida. She had the local habit of placing the word 'eh' at the end of her remarks, questions and answers alike.

'I'll say, man,' said Isa, for she also used the common currency, adding 'man' to most of the statements she addressed to man and woman alike.

'You'll be going to the Stardust,' said Mrs. Jan Cloote. 'Won't you now, Isa?'

'The Stardust!' said Mrs. Marais, the insurance agent's wife. 'You surely don't mean the nightclub, man?'

'Why, yes,' said Mrs. Jan Cloote in her precise voice. She alone of the family did not use the local idiom, and in fact her speech had improved since her Somerset days. 'Why, yes,' she said, 'she enjoys herself, why not?'

'Only young once, eh?' said the young man, putting ash in his saucer as Mrs. Jan Cloote frowned at him.

Mrs. Jan Cloote sent Maida upstairs to fetch some of Isa's presents, things she had been given by men; evening bags, brooches, silk stockings. It was rather awkward. What could one say?

'They are very nice,' I said.

'This is nothing, nothing,' said Mrs. Jan Cloote, 'nothing to the things she could get. But she only goes with the nice fellows.'

'And do you dance too?' I enquired of Greta.

'No, man,' she said. 'Isa does it for us, eh. Isa dances lovely.'

'You said it, man,' said Maida.

'Ah yes,' sighed Mrs. Jan Cloote, 'we're quiet folk. We would have a dull life of it, if it wasn't for Isa.'

'She needs taking care of, that child,' said Mrs. Marais.

'Isa!' said her mother. 'Do you hear Mrs. Marais, what she says?'

'I do, man,' said Isa. 'I do, eh.'

From my room it was impossible not to overhear all that was going on in the pawnshop, just beneath my window.

'I hope it doesn't disturb you,' said Mrs. Jan Cloote, with a sideways glance at her two elder daughters.

'No,' I thought it best to say, 'I don't hear a thing.'

'I always tell the girls,' said Mrs. Jan Cloote, 'that there is nothing to be ashamed of, being a P.B.'

31

'A P.B.?' asked the young clerk, who had a friend who played the drums in the Police Band.

Mrs. Jan Cloote lowered her voice. 'A *pawn broker*,' she informed him rapidly.

'That's right,' said the young man.

'There's nothing to be ashamed of in it,' said Mrs. Jan Cloote. 'And of course I'm only down as a P.B.'s *wife*, not a P.B.'

'We keep the shop beautiful, man,' said Maida.

'Have you seen it?' Mrs. Jan Cloote asked me.

'No,' I said.

'Well, there's nothing to see inside, really,' she said; 'but some P.B. shops are a sight enough. You should see some of the English ones. The dirt!'

'Or so I'm told,' she added.

'They *are* very rough-and-tumble in England,' I admitted.

'Why,' said Mrs. Jan Cloote, 'have you been inside one?'

'Oh, yes, quite a few,' I said, pausing to recollect; ' . . . in London, of course, and then there was one in Manchester, and——'

'But what for, man?' said Greta.

'To pawn things,' I said, glad to impress them with my knowledge of their trade. 'There was my compass,' I said, 'but I never saw *that* again. Not that I ever used the thing.'

Mrs. Jan Cloote put down her cup and looked round the room to see if everyone had unfortunately heard me. She was afraid they had.

'Thank God,' she said; 'touch wood I have never had to do it.'

'I can't say that I've ever popped anything, myself,' said Mrs. Marais.

'My poor mother used to take things now and again,' said Mr. Marais.

'I daresay,' said Mrs. Marais.

'We get some terrible scum coming in,' said the pawnbroker's wife.

'I'm going to the P.B.'s dinner-dance,' said Isa. 'What'll I way?' she added, meaning what would she wear. The girls did not pronounce the final 'r' in certain words.

'You can way your midnight blue,' said Greta.

'No,' said her mother, 'no, no, no. She'll have to get a new dress.'

'I'm going to get my hay cut short,' announced Isa, indicating her yellow pigtails.

Her mother squirmed with excitement at the prospect. Greta and Maida blushed, with a strange and greedy look.

At last the door was opened a few inches and we were allowed to file out, one by one.

Next morning as usual I heard Mrs. Jan Cloote opening up the pawnshop. She dealt expertly with the customers who, as usual, waited on the doorstep. Once the first rush was over, business generally became easier as the day progressed. But for the first half-hour the bell tinkled incessantly as sailors and other troops arrived, anxious to deposit cameras, cigarette cases, watches, suits of clothes and other things which, like my compass, would never be redeemed. Though I could not see her, it was easy to visualise what actions accompanied the words I could hear so well; Mrs. Jan Cloote would, I supposed,

33

examine the proffered article for about three minutes
(this would account for a silence which followed her
opening 'Well?'). The examination would be con-
ducted with utter intensity, seeming to have its sensi-
tive point, its assessing faculty, in her long nose. (I had
already seen her perform this feat with Isa's treasures.)
She would not smell the thing, actually; but it would
appear to be her nose which calculated and finally
judged. Then she would sharply name her figure.
If this evoked a protest, she would become really
eloquent; though never unreasonable, at this stage. A
list of the object's defects would proceed like ticker
tape from the mouth of Mrs. Jan Cloote; its depre-
ciating market value was known to her; this suit of
clothes would never fit another man; that ring was
not worth the melting. Usually, the pawners accepted
her offer, after she ceased. If not, the pawnbroker's
wife turned to the next customer without further
comment. 'Well?' she would say to the next one.
Should the first-comer still linger, hesitant, per-
plexed, it was then that Mrs. Jan Cloote became
unreasonable in tone. 'Haven't you made up your
mind yet?' she would demand. 'What are you waiting
for, what are you waiting for?' The effect of this
shock treatment was either the swift disappearance
of the customer, or his swift clinching of the bargain.

Like most establishments in those parts, Mrs. Jan
Cloote's pawnshop was partitioned off into sections,
rather like a public house with its saloon, public and
private bars. These compartments separated white
customers from black, and black from those known
as coloured — the Indians, Malays and half-castes.

Whenever someone with a tanned face came in at

the white entrance, Mrs. Jan Cloote always gave the customer the benefit of the doubt. But she would complain wearily of this to Maida and Greta as she rushed back and forth.

'Did you see that coloured girl that went out?' she would say. 'Came in the white way. Oh, coloured, of course she was coloured but you daren't say anything. We'd be up for slander.'

This particular morning, trade was pressing. A troopship had come in.

'Now *that* was a coloured,' said Mrs. Jan Cloote in a lull between shop bells. 'He came in the white way.'

'I'd have kicked his behind,' said Isa.

'Listen to Isa, eh!' giggled Maida.

'Isa's the one!' said the mother, as she rushed away again, summoned by the bell.

This time the voices came from another part of the shop set aside from the rest. I had noticed, from the outside, that it was marked 'OFFICE — PRIVATE'.

'Oh, it's you?' said Mrs. Jan Cloote.

'That picture,' said the voice. 'Here's the ticket.'

'A month late,' she said. 'You've lost it.'

'Here's the fifteen bob,' said the man.

'No, no,' she said. 'It's too late. You haven't paid up the interest; it's gone.'

'I'll pay up the interest now,' he said. 'Come now,' he said, 'we're old friends and you promised to keep it for me.'

'My grandfather painted that picture,' he said.

'You promised to keep it for me,' he said.

'Not for a month,' she said at last. 'Not for a whole month. It was only worth the price of the frame.'

'It's a good picture,' he said.

'A terrible picture,' she said. 'Who would want a picture like that? It might bring us bad luck. I've thrown it away.'

'Listen, old dear——' he began.

'Out!' she said. 'Outside!'

'I'm staying here,' he said, 'till I get my picture.'

'Maida! Greta!' she called.

'All right,' he said, hopeless and lost. 'I'm going.'

A week later Mrs. Jan Cloote caught me in the hall again. 'A *little* cup of tea,' she whispered. 'Come in for a chat, just with ourselves and young Mr. Fleming, tonight.'

It was imperative to attend these periodic tea sittings. Those of Mrs. Jan Cloote's lodgers who did not attend, suffered many discomforts; rooms were not cleaned nor beds made; morning tea was brought up cold and newspapers not at all. It was difficult to find rooms at that time. 'Thank you,' I said.

I joined the family that night. The Marais couple had left, but I found the young clerk there. Isa came in, painted up as before.

There was one addition to the room; a picture on the wall. It was dreadful as a piece of work, at the same time as it was fascinating on account of the period it stood for. The date of this period would be about the mid-eighteen-nineties. It represented a girl bound to a railway line. Her blue sash fluttered across her body, and her hands were raised in anguish to her head, where the hair, yellow and abundant, was spreading over the rails around her. Twenty yards away was a bend on the rail-track. A train approached this bend, full-steam. The driver could not see the girl. As you know, the case was hopeless. A moment, and she would be pulp. But wait! A motor-car, one of the first of its kind, was approaching a level crossing nearby. A group of young men, out for a joy-ride, were loaded into this high, bright vehicle. One of them had seen the girl's plight. This Johnnie was standing on the seat, waving his motoring cap high above his head and pointing to her. His companions were just on the point of realising what had happened. Would they be in time to rescue her? — to stop the onrushing train? Of course not. The perspective of the picture told me this clearly enough. There was not a chance for the girl. And anyhow, I reflected, she lies there for as long as the picture lasts; the train approaches; the young mashers in their brand-new automobile — they are always on the point of seeing before them the girl tied to the rails, her hair spread around her, the ridiculous sash waving about, and her hands uplifted to her head.

On the whole, I liked the picture. It was the proto-type of so many other paintings of its kind; and the prototype, the really typical object, is something I rarely have a chance of seeing.

'You're looking at Isa's picture,' said Mrs. Jan Cloote.

'It's a very wonderful picture,' she declared. 'A very famous English artist flew out on a Sunderland on purpose to paint Isa. The R.A.F. let him have the plane and all the crew so that he could come. As soon as they saw Isa's photo at the Raf Headquarters in London, they told the artist to take the Sunderland.'

'He put Isa in that pose, doing her hair,' Mrs. Jan Cloote continued, gazing fondly at the picture.

I said nothing. Nor did the young clerk. I tried looking at the picture with my head on one side, and, indeed, the girl bore a slight resemblance to Isa; the distracted hands around her head did look rather as if she were doing her hair. Of course, to get this effect, one had to ignore the train, and the motor-car and the other details. I decided that the picture would be about fifty years old. Undoubtedly, it was not recent.

'What do you think of it?' said Mrs. Jan Cloote.

'Very nice,' I said.

The young clerk was silent.

'You're very quiet tonight, Mr. Fleming,' said Maida.

He gave a jerky laugh which nearly knocked over his cup.

'I saw Mrs. Marais today,' he ventured.

'Oh, her,' said Mrs. Jan Cloote. 'Did you speak?'

'Certainly not,' he said; 'I just passed her by.'

'Quite right,' said Mrs. Jan Cloote.

'I gave them notice,' she explained to me. 'Mr. wasn't so bad, but Mrs. was the worst tenant I've ever had.'

'The things she said!' Greta added.

'I showed her every consideration,' said the pawnbroker's wife, 'and all I got was insults.'

'Insults,' Mr. Fleming said.

'Mr. Fleming was here when it happened,' said Mrs. Jan Cloote.

'We were showing her Isa's picture,' she continued, 'and do you believe it, she said it wasn't Isa at all. To my face she as good as called me a liar, didn't she, Mr. Fleming?'

'That's true,' said Mr. Fleming, examining a tea-leaf on his spoon.

'Mr. Marais, of course, was in an awkward position,' said Mrs. Jan Cloote. 'You see, he's right under his wife's thumb, and he didn't dare contradict her. He only said there might be some mistake. But she sat on him at once. "*That's* not Isa", she said.'

'Poor Mr. Marais!' said Greta.

'I'm sorry for Mr. Marais,' said Maida.

'He's soft in the head, man,' said Isa.

'Isa's a real scream,' said her mother when she had recovered from her gust of laughter. 'And she's right. Old Marais isn't all there.'

'What was it again?' she enquired of the young clerk. 'What was it again, that old Marais told you afterwards, about Isa's picture?'

The young clerk looked at me, and quickly looked away.

'What did Mr. Marais say about the picture?' I said insistently.

'Well,' said Mr. Fleming, 'I don't really remember.'

'Now, you remember all right,' said Mrs. Jan Cloote. 'Come on, give us a laugh.'

'Oh, he only said,' Mr. Fleming replied, gazing manfully at the painting, 'he only said there were railway lines and a train in the picture.'

'*Only* said!' Mrs. Jan Cloote put in.

'Well, poor thing,' said Mr. Fleming; 'he can't help it, I suppose. He's mad.'

'And didn't he say there was an old-fashioned car in the picture, man?' said Greta. 'That's what you told us, man.'

'Yes,' said the clerk, with a giggle, 'he said that too.'

39

'So you see,' said Mrs. Jan Cloote. 'The man's out of his mind. A railway in Isa's picture! I laugh every time I think of it.'

'As for Mrs. Marais,' she added; 'as for *her*, I never trusted the woman from the start. "Mrs. Marais," said I, "you'll take a week's notice." And they left the next day.'

'Good riddance to the old bitch,' said Isa.

'She was jealous of Isa's picture, eh,' chuckled Greta.

'We had a nice time with the artist, though, when he was painting Isa,' said Mrs. Jan Cloote.

'I'll say, man,' said Maida, 'and the crew as well.'

'We often have famous artists here,' said the mother, 'don't we?'

'We do, man,' said Greta. 'They come after Isa.'

'And the crew,' said Maida. 'They was nice. But the pilot did a real man's trick on Isa.'

'Yes, the swine,' said the mother. 'But never mind, Isa's got other boys. Isa could go on the films.'

'Isa would be great on the films,' said Greta.

'All the famous actors come here,' said Mrs. Jan Cloote. 'We get all the actors. They want Isa for the films. But we wouldn't let her go on the films.'

'She'd be a star, man,' said Greta.

'But we wouldn't let her go on the films,' Maida said.

'She'll do what she likes,' said the mother, 'when she leaves school.'

'Bloody right,' said Isa.

'You know Max Melville?' said Mrs. Jan Cloote to me.

'I've *heard* the name . . .' I said warily.

'Heard the *name*! Why, Max Melville's a top-ranking

40

star! He was here after Isa the other day. Isn't that right, Greta?'

'Sure,' said Greta.

And Mrs. Jan Cloote took up the story again. 'I told him there was too much publicity on the films for Isa. "We're quiet folk, Max," I said. '*Max*, I called him, just like that.'

'Max was a rare guy,' said Maida.

'He gave Isa a wonderful present,' said Mrs. Jan Cloote. 'Not that it's worth much, but it belonged to his family and it's got the sentimental value, and he wouldn't have parted with it to anyone else but Isa. Run upstairs and fetch it, Maida.'

Maida hesitated. 'Was it that brooch . . .?' she began.

'No,' said her mother sorrowfully and slowly. 'Isa got the brooch from the artist. I'm surprised at you forgetting what Max Melville gave to Isa.'

'I'll get it,' said Greta, jumping up.

She returned presently, with a small compass in her hand.

'It isn't worth much,' Mrs. Jan Cloote was saying as she handed it round. 'But Max's great-grandfather was an explorer, and he had this very compass on him when he crossed the Himalayas. He never came back, but the compass was found on his body. So it was very very precious to Maxie, but he parted with it to Isa.'

I had been given the compass when I was fourteen; it was new then; I recognized it immediately, and, while Mrs. Jan Cloote was talking, I recognized it more and more. The scratches and dents which I make on my own possessions are always familiar to me, like my own signature. . . .

'A very old antique compass,' said the pawnbroker's wife, passing her hand over its face appraisingly. 'It was nice of Max Melville to give it away. But of course he wanted Isa for the films, and that may have been the reason.'

'What do you think of it?' she asked me.

'Very interesting,' I said.

What voyager had fetched it over the seas? How many hands had it passed through in its passage from the pawnshop where I had pledged it, to the pawnshop of Mrs. Jan Cloote? I wondered these things, and also, why it was that I didn't really mind seeing my compass caressed by the hands of this pawnbroker's wife — seeing it made to serve her pleasure. I didn't care. Her nose pointed towards it, as to a North. . . .

'We shall never part with this,' Mrs. Jan Cloote was saying; 'because of the sentimental reason, you know. It wouldn't fetch a price, of course.'

I had, for a few years, kept the compass lying about amongst my things, until the day came to pawn it. That was how it had got scratched and knocked about. It was knocked about in the drawer, thrown aside always, because I was looking for something else. I had never used the compass, never taken my bearings by it. Perhaps it had never been very much used at all. The marks of wear upon it were mainly those I had made. Whoever had pledged it at Mrs. Jan Cloote's pawnshop did not think enough of it to redeem it. The pawnbroker's wife was welcome to the compass, for it was truly hers.

'It wouldn't fetch a price,' said Mrs. Jan Cloote. 'Not that we think of the price; it's the thought that matters.'

'It's Isa's lucky mascot,' said Maida. 'You'll have to take it with you when you go to Hollywood, Isa, man.'

'Hollywood!' said Mrs. Jan Cloote. 'Oh, no, no. If Isa goes on the pictures she'll go to an English studio. There's too much publicity in Hollywood. Do you see our Isa in Hollywood, Mr. Fleming?'

'Not exactly,' said the young man.

'I'd be great in Hollywood, man,' said young Isa.

'Well, maybe . . .' said the mother.

'Yes, maybe,' said Mr. Fleming.

'But there's too much show in Hollywood,' said Isa.

'You see,' said Mrs. Jan Cloote, turning to me, 'we're quiet people. We keep ourselves to ourselves, and as Mr. Fleming was saying the other day, we live in quite a world of our own, don't we, Mr. Fleming?'

They opened the door and let me sidle through, into the dark hall.

The Twins

WHEN Jennie was at school with me, she was one of those well-behaved and intelligent girls who were, and maybe still are, popular with everyone in Scottish schools. The popularity of boys and girls in English schools so far as I gather, goes by other, less easily definable qualities, and also by their prowess at games. However, it was not so with us, and although Jennie was not much use at hockey, she was good and quiet and clever, and we all liked her. She was rather nice-looking too, plump, dark-haired, clear, neat.

She married a Londoner, Simon Reeves. I heard from her occasionally. She was living in Essex, and once or twice, when she came to London, we met. But it was some years before I could pay my long-promised visit to them, and by the time I got round to it, her twins, Marjie and Jeff, were five years old.

They were noticeably beautiful children; dark, like Jennie, with a charming way of holding their heads. Jennie was, as she always had been, a sensible girl. She made nothing of their beauty, on which everyone felt compelled to remark. 'As long as they behave themselves ——' said Jennie; and I thought what a pretty girl she was herself, and how little notice she took of her looks, and how much care she took with other people. I noticed that Jennie assumed that everyone else was inwardly as quiet, as peacefully inclined, as

44

little prone to be perturbed, as herself. I found this very restful and was grateful to Jennie for it. Her husband resembled her in this; but otherwise, Simon was more positive. He was brisk, full of activity, as indeed was Jennie; the difference between them was that Jennie never appeared to be bustling, even at her busiest hours, while Simon always seemed to live in the act of doing something. They were a fine match. I supposed he had gained from Jennie, during their six years of marriage, a little of her sweet and self-denying nature for he was really considerate. Simon would stop mowing the lawn at once, if he caught sight of the old man next door asleep in a deck-chair, although his need to do something about the lawn was apparently intense. For Jennie's part, she had learned from Simon how to speak to men without embarrassment. This was something she had been unable to do at the age of eighteen. Jennie got from Simon an insight into the mentalities of a fair variety of people, because his friends were curiously mixed, socially and intellectually. And in a way, Simon bore within himself an integrated combination of all those people he brought to the house; he represented them, almost, and kept his balance at the same time. So that Jennie derived from Simon a knowledge of the world, without actually weathering the world. A happy couple. And then, of course, there were the twins.

I arrived on a Saturday afternoon, to spend a week. The lovely twins were put to bed at six, and I did not see them much on the Sunday, as a neighbouring couple took them off for a day's picnicking with their own children. I spent most of Monday chatting with Jennie about old times and new times, while little Marjie and

Jeff played in the garden. They were lively, full of noise and everything that goes with healthy children. And they were advanced for their years; both could read and write, taught by Jennie. She was sending them to school in September. They pronounced their words very clearly, and I was amused to notice some of Jennie's Scottish phraseology coming out in their English intonation.

Well, they went off to bed at six sharp that day: Simon came home shortly afterwards, and we dined in a pleasant hum-drum peace.

It wasn't until the Tuesday morning that I really got on close speaking terms with the twins. Jennie took the car to the village to fetch some groceries, and for an hour I played with them in the garden. Again, I was struck by their loveliness and intelligence, especially of the little girl. She was the sort of child who noticed everything. The boy was quicker with words, however; his vocabulary was exceptionally large.

Jennie returned, and after tea, I went indoors to write letters. I heard Jennie telling the children 'Go and play yourselves down the other end of the garden and don't make too much noise, mind'. She went to do something in the kitchen. After a while, there was a ring at the back door. The children scampered in from the garden, while Jennie answered the ring.

'Baker,' said the man.

'Oh, yes,' said Jennie: 'wait, I'll get my purse.'

I went on writing my letter, only half-hearing the sound of Jennie's small-change as she, presumably, paid the baker's man.

In a moment, Marjie was by my side.

'Hallo,' I said.

Marjie did not answer.

'Hallo, Marjie,' I said. 'Have you come to keep me company?'

'Listen,' said little Marjie in a whisper, looking over her shoulder. 'Listen.'

'Yes,' I said.

She looked over her shoulder again, as if afraid her mother might come in.

'Will you give me half-a-crown?' whispered Marjie, holding out her hand.

'Well,' I said, 'what do you want it for?'

'I want it,' said Marjie, looking furtively behind her again.

'Would your mummy want you to have it?' I said.

'Give me half-a-crown,' said Marjie.

'I'd rather not,' I said. 'But I'll tell you what, I'll buy you a——'

But Marjie had fled, out of the door, into the kitchen. 'She'd rather not,' I heard her say to someone.

Presently, Jennie came in, looking upset.

'Oh,' she said, 'I hope you didn't feel hurt. I only wanted to pay the baker, and I hadn't enough change. He hadn't any either; so just on the spur of the moment I sent Marjie for a loan of half-a-crown till tonight. But I shouldn't have done it. I *never* borrow anything as a rule.'

'Well, of course!' I said. 'Of course I'll lend you half-a-crown. I've got plenty of change. I didn't understand and I got the message all wrong; I thought she wanted it for herself and that you wouldn't like that.'

Jennie looked doubtful. I funked explaining the whole of Marjie's act. It isn't easy to give evidence against a child of five.

'Oh, they never ask for money,' said Jennie. 'I would never allow them to ask anyone for anything. They never do *that*.'

'I'm sure they don't,' I said, floundering a bit.

Jennie was much too kind to point out that this was what I had just been suggesting. She was altogether too nice to let the incident make any difference during my stay. That night, Simon came home just after six. He had bought two elaborate spinning-tops for the twins. These tops had to be wound up, and they sang a tinny little tune while they spun.

'You'll ruin those children,' said Jennie.

Simon enjoyed himself that evening, playing with the tops.

'You'll break them before the children even see them,' said Jennie.

Simon put them away. But when one of his friends, a pilot from a nearby aerodrome, looked in later in the evening, Simon brought out the tops again; and the two men played delightedly with them, occasionally peering into the works and discussing what made the tops go; while Jennie and I made scornful comments.

Little Marjie and Jeff were highly pleased with the tops next morning, but by the afternoon they had tired of them and gone on to something more in the romping line. After dinner Simon produced a couple of small gadgets. They were the things that go inside musical cigarette-boxes, he explained, and he thought they would fit into the spinning-tops, so that the children could have a change of tune.

'When they get fed up with *Pop Goes the Weasel*,' he said, 'they can have *In and Out the Windows*.'

He got out one of the tops to take it apart and fit in

the new tune. But when he had put the pieces together again, the top wouldn't sing at all. Jennie tried to help, but we couldn't get *In and Out the Windows*. So Simon patiently unpieced the top, put the gadgets aside, and said they would do for something else.

'That's Jeff's top,' said Jennie, in her precise way, looking at the pieces on the carpet. 'Jeff's is the red one, Marjie has the blue.'

Once more, Simon started piecing the toy together, with the old tune inside it, while Jennie and I went to make some tea.

'I'll bet it won't work now,' said Jennie with a giggle.

When we returned, Simon was reading and the top was gone.

'Did you fix it?' said Jennie.

'Yes,' he said absently. 'I've put it away.'

It rained the next morning and the twins were indoors.

'Why not play with your tops?' Jennie said.

'Your Daddy took one of them to pieces last night,' Jennie informed them, 'and put all the pieces back again.'

Jennie had the stoic in her nature and did not believe in shielding her children from possible disappointment.

'He was hoping,' she added, 'to fit new tunes inside it. But it wouldn't work with the new tune. . . . But he's going to try again.'

They took this quite hopefully, and I didn't see much of them for some hours although, when the rain stopped and I went outside, I saw the small boy spinning his bright-red top on the hard concrete of the garage floor. About noon little Jeff came running into the kitchen where Jennie was baking. He was howling hard, his

small face distorted with grief. He held in both arms
the spare parts of his top.

'My top!' he sobbed. 'My top!'

'Goodness,' said Jennie, 'what did you do to it?
Don't cry, poor wee pet.'

'I found it,' he said. 'I found my top all in pieces
under that box behind Daddy's car.

'My top,' he wept. 'Daddy's broken my top.'
Marjie came in and looked on unmoved, hugging her
blue top.

'But you were playing with the top this morning!' I
said. 'Isn't yours the red one? You were spinning it.'

'I was playing with the blue one,' he wept. 'And
then I found my own top all broken. Daddy broke
it.'

Jennie sat them up to their dinner, and Jeff presently
stopped crying.

Jennie was cheerful about it, although she said to me
afterwards, 'I think Simon might have told me he
couldn't put it together again. But isn't it just like a
man? They're that proud of themselves, men.'

As I have said, it isn't easy to give evidence against a
child of five. And especially, to its mother.

Jennie tactfully put the pieces of the top back in the
box behind the garage. They were still there, rusty and
untouched, in a pile of other rusty things, seven years
later, for I saw them. Jennie got skipping ropes for
the twins that day and when they had gone to bed,
she removed Marjie's top from the toy-cupboard. 'It'll
only make wee Jeff cry to see it,' she said to me. 'We'll
just forget about the tops.

'And I don't want Simon to find out that I found
him out,' she giggled.

I don't think tops were ever mentioned again in the household. If they were, I am sure Jennie would change the subject. An affectionate couple; it was impossible not to feel kindly towards them; not so, towards the children.

I was abroad for some years after that, and heard sometimes from Jennie at first; later, we seldom wrote, and then not at all. I had been back in London for about a year when I met Jennie in Baker Street. She was excited about her children, now aged twelve, who had both won scholarships and were going off to boarding schools in the autumn.

'Come and see them while they've got their holidays,' she said. 'We often talk about you, Simon and I.' It was good to hear Jennie's kind voice again.

I went to stay for a few days in August. I felt sure the twins must have grown out of their peculiarities, and I was right. Jennie brought them to meet me at the station. They had grown rather quiet; both still extremely good-looking. These children possessed an unusual composure for their years. They were well-mánnered as Jennie had been at their age, but without Jennie's shyness.

Simon was pruning something in the garden when we got to the house.

'Why, you haven't changed a bit,' he said. 'A bit thinner maybe. Nice to see you so flourishing.'

Jennie went to make tea. In these surroundings she seemed to have endured no change; and she had made no change in her ways in the seven years since my last visit.

The twins started chatting about their school life, and Simon asked me questions I could not answer about the size of the population of the places I had lived in abroad. When Jennie returned, Simon leapt off to wash.

'I'm sorry Simon said that,' said Jennie to me when he had gone. 'I don't think he should have said it, but you know how tactless men are?'

'Said what?' I asked.

'About you looking thin and ill,' said Jennie.

'Oh, I didn't take it *that* way!' I said.

'Didn't you?' said Jennie with an understanding smile. 'That was sweet of you.

'Thin and haggard indeed!' said Jennie as she poured out the tea, and the twins discreetly passed the sandwiches.

That night I sat up late talking to the couple. Jennie retained the former habit of making a tea-session at nine o'clock and I accompanied her to the kitchen. While she was talking, she packed a few biscuits neatly into a small green box.

'There's the kettle boiling,' said Jennie, going out with the box in her hand. 'You know where the teapot is. I won't be a minute.'

She returned in a few seconds, and we carried off our tray.

It was past one before we parted for the night. Jennie had taken care to make me comfortable. She had put fresh flowers on the dressing-table, and there, beside my bed, was the little box of biscuits she had thoughtfully provided. I munched one while I looked out of the window at the calm country sky, ruminating upon Jennie's perennial merits. I have always regarded the lack of neurosis in people with awe. I am too much with brightly intelligent, highly erratic friends. In this

Jennie, I decided, reposed a mystery which I and my like could not fathom.

Jennie had driven off next day to fetch the twins from a swimming-pool nearby, when Simon came home from his office.

'I'm glad Jennie's out,' he said, 'for I wanted a chance to talk to you.

'I hope you won't mind,' he said, 'but Jennie's got a horror of mice.'

'Mice?' I said.

'Yes,' said Simon, 'so don't eat biscuits in your room if you wouldn't mind. Jennie was rather upset when she saw the crumbs but of course she'd have a fit if she knew I'd told you. She'd die rather than tell you. But there it is, and I know you'll understand.'

'But Jennie put the biscuits in my room herself,' I explained. 'She packed them in a box and took them up last night.'

Simon looked worried. 'We've had mice before,' he said, 'and she can't bear the thought of them upstairs.'

'Jennie put the biscuits there,' I insisted, feeling all in the wrong.

'And,' I said, 'I saw Jennie pack the box. I'll ask her about it.'

'*Please*,' said Simon, 'please don't do that. She would be so hurt to think I'd spoken about it. Please,' he said, 'go on eating biscuits in your room; I shouldn't have mentioned it.'

Of course I promised not to eat any more of the things. And Simon, with a knowing smile, said he would give me larger helpings at dinner, so that I wouldn't go hungry.

The biscuit-box had gone when I went to my room.

Jennie was busy all next day preparing for a cocktail-party they were giving that night. The twins devotedly gave up their day to the cutting of sandwiches and the making of curious patterns with small pieces of anchovy on diminutive squares of toast.

Jennie wanted some provisions from the village, and I offered to fetch them. I took the car, and noticed it was almost out of petrol; I got some on the way. When I returned, these good children were eating their supper standing up in the kitchen, and without a word of protest, cleared off to bed before the guests arrived.

When Simon came home I met him in the hall. He was uneasy about the gin; he thought there might not be enough. He decided to go straight to the local and get more.

'And,' he said, 'I've just remembered. The car's almost out of petrol. I promised to drive the Rawlings' home after the party. I nearly forgot. I'll get some petrol too.'

'Oh, I got some to-day,' I said.

There were ten guests, four married couples and two unattached girls. Jennie and I did the handing round of snacks and Simon did the drinks. His speciality was a cocktail he had just discovered, called Loopamp. This Loopamp required him to make frequent excursions to the kitchen for replenishments of prune-juice and ice. Simon persuaded himself that Loopamp was in great demand among the guests. We all drank it obligingly. As he took his shakers to the kitchen for the fourth time, he called out to one of the unattached girls who was standing by the door, 'Mollie, bring that lemon-jug too, will you?'

Mollie followed him with the lemon-jug.

'Very good scholarships,' Jennie was saying to an elderly man. 'Jeff came fourth among the boys, and Marjie took eleventh place in the girls. There were only fourteen scholarships, so she was lucky. If it hadn't been for the geography she'd have been near the top. Her English teacher told me.'

'Really!' said the man.

'Yes,' said Jennie. 'Mollie Thomas; you know Mollie Thomas. That's Marjie's English mistress. She's here to-night. Where's Mollie?' said Jennie, looking round.

'She's in the kitchen,' I said.

'Making Loopamp, I expect,' said Jennie. 'What a name, Loopamp!'

Simon and Jennie looked rather jaded the next morning. I put it down to the Loopamp. They had very little to say, and when Simon had left for London, I asked Jennie how she was feeling.

'Not too good,' she said. 'Not too good. I am really sorry, my dear, about the petrol. I wish you had asked me for the money. Now, here it is, and don't say another word. Simon's so touchy.'

'Touchy?'

'Well,' said Jennie; 'you know what men are like. I wish you had come to me about it. You know how scrupulous I am about debts. And so is Simon. He just didn't know you had got the petrol, and, of course, he couldn't understand why you felt hurt.'

I sent myself a wire that morning, summoning myself back to London. There wasn't a train before the 6.30, but I caught this. Simon arrived home as I was getting into the taxi, and he joined Jennie and the children on the doorstep to wave goodbye.

'Mind you come again soon,' said Jennie.

As I waved back, I noticed that the twins, who were waving to me, were not looking at me, but at their parents. There was an expression on their faces which I have only seen once before. That was at the Royal Academy, when I saw a famous portrait-painter standing bemused, giving a remarkable and long look at the work of his own hands. So, with wonder, pride and bewilderment, did the twins gaze upon Jennie and Simon.

I wrote and thanked them, avoiding any reference to future meetings. By return I had a letter from Simon. 'I am sorry,' he wrote, 'that you got the impression that Mollie and I were behaving improperly in the kitchen on the night of our party. Jennie was very upset. She does not, of course, doubt my fidelity, but she is distressed that you could suggest such a thing. It was very embarrassing for Jennie to hear it in front of all her friends, and I hope, for Jennie's sake, you will not mention to her that I have written you about it. Jennie would rather die than hurt your feelings. Yours ever, Simon Reeves.'

Miss Pinkerton's Apocalypse

ONE evening, a damp one in February, something flew in at the window. Miss Laura Pinkerton, who was doing something innocent to the fire, heard a faint throbbing noise overhead. On looking up, 'George! come here! come quickly!'

George Lake came in at once, though sullenly because of their quarrel, eating a sandwich from the kitchen. He looked up at the noise then sat down immediately.

From this point onward their story comes in two versions, his and hers. But they agree as to the main facts; they agree that it was a small round flattish object, and that it flew.

'It's a flying object of some sort,' whispered George eventually.

'It's a saucer,' said Miss Pinkerton, keen and loud, 'an antique piece. You can tell by the shape.'

'It can't be an antique, that's absolutely certain,' George said.

He ought to have been more tactful, and would have been, but for the stress of the moment. Of course it set Miss Pinkerton off, she being in the right.

'I know my facts,' she stated as usual, 'I should hope I know my facts. I've been in antique china for twenty-three years in the autumn,' which was true, and George knew it.

The little saucer was cavorting round the lamp.

'It seems to be attracted by the light,' George re-marked, as one might distinguish a moth.

Promptly, it made as if to dive dangerously at George's head. He ducked, and Miss Pinkerton backed against the wall. As the dish tilted on its side, skim-ming George's shoulder, Miss Pinkerton could see inside it.

'The thing might be radio-active. It might be dan-gerous.' George was breathless. The saucer had climbed, was circling high above his head, and now made for him again, but missed.

'It is not radio-active,' said Miss Pinkerton, 'it is Spode.'

'Don't be so damn silly,' George replied, under the stress of the occasion.

'All right, very well,' said Miss Pinkerton, 'it is not Spode. I suppose you are the expert, George, I suppose you know best. I was only judging by the pattern. After the best part of a lifetime in china——'

'It must be a forgery,' George said unfortunately. For, unfortunately, something familiar and abrasive in Miss Pinkerton's speech began to grind within him. Also, he was afraid of the saucer.

It had taken a stately turn, following the picture rail in a steady career round the room.

'Forgery, ha!' said Miss Pinkerton. She was out of the room like a shot, and in again carrying a pair of steps.

'I will examine the mark,' said she, pointing intensely at the saucer. 'Where are my glasses?'

Obligingly, the saucer settled in a corner; it hung like a spider a few inches from the ceiling. Miss Pinkerton adjusted the steps. With her glasses on she was almost her sunny self again, she was ceremonious and expert.

'Don't touch it, don't go near it!' George pushed her aside and grabbed the steps, knocking over a blue glass bowl, a Dresden figure, a vase of flowers and a decanter of sherry; like a bull in a china shop, as Miss Pinkerton exclaimed. But she was determined, and struggled to reclaim the steps.

'Laura!' he said desperately. 'I believe it is Spode. I take your word.'

The saucer then flew out of the window.

They acted quickly. They telephoned to the local paper. A reporter would come right away. Meanwhile, Miss Pinkerton telephoned to her two scientific friends — at least, one was interested in psychic research and the other was an electrician. But she got no reply from either. George had leaned out of the window, scanning the rooftops and the night sky. He had leaned out of the back windows, had tried all the lights and the wireless. These things were as usual.

The news man arrived, accompanied by a photographer.

'There's nothing to photograph,' said Miss Pinkerton excitably. 'It went away.'

'We could take a few shots of the actual spot,' the man explained.

Miss Pinkerton looked anxiously at the result of George and the steps.

'The place is a wreck.'

Sherry from the decanter was still dripping from the sideboard.

'I'd better clear the place up. George, help me!' She

fluttered nervously, and started to pack the fire with small coals.

'No, leave everything as it is,' the reporter advised her. 'Did the apparition make this mess?'

George and Miss Pinkerton spoke together.

'Well, indirectly,' said George.

'It wasn't an apparition,' said Miss Pinkerton.

The reporter settled on the nearest chair, poising his pencil and asking, 'Do you mind if I take notes?'

'Would you mind sitting over here?' said Miss Pinkerton. 'I don't use the Queen Annes normally. They are very frail pieces.'

The reporter rose as if stung, then perched on a table which Miss Pinkerton looked at uneasily.

'You see, I'm in antiques,' she rattled on, for the affair was beginning to tell on her, as George told himself. In fact he sized up that she was done for; his irritation abated, his confidence came flooding back.

'Now, Laura, sit down and take it easy.' Solicitously he pushed her into an easy chair.

'She's overwrought,' he informed the pressmen in an audible undertone.

'You say this object actually flew in this window?' suggested the reporter.

'That is correct,' said George.

The camera-man trained his apparatus on the window.

'And you were both here at the time?'

'No,' Miss Pinkerton said. 'Mr. Lake was in the kitchen and I called out, of course. But he didn't see inside the bowl, only the outside, underneath where the manufacturer's mark is. I saw the pattern so I got the steps to make sure. That's how Mr. Lake knocked my things over. I saw inside.'

'I am going to say something,' said George.

The men looked hopefully towards him. After a pause, George continued, 'Let us begin at the beginning.'

'Right,' said the reporter, breezing up.

'It was like this,' George said. 'I came straight in when Miss Pinkerton screamed, and there was a white convex disc, you realize, floating around up there.'

The reporter contemplated the spot indicated by George.

'It was making a hell of a racket like a cat purring,' George told him.

'Any idea what it really was?' the reporter enquired.

George took his time to answer. 'Well, yes,' he said, 'and no.'

'Spode ware,' said Miss Pinkerton.

George continued, 'I'm not up in these things. I'm extremely sceptical as a rule. This was a new experience to me.'

'That's just it,' said Miss Pinkerton. 'Personally, I've been in china for twenty-three years. I recognised the thing immediately.'

The reporter scribbled and enquired, 'These flying discs appear frequently in China?'

'It was a saucer. I've never seen one flying before,' Miss Pinkerton explained.

'I am going to ask a question,' George said.

Miss Pinkerton continued, 'Mr. Lake is an art framer. He handles old canvases but next to no antiques.'

61

'I am going to ask. Are you telling the story or am
I?' George said.

'Perhaps Mr. Lake's account first and then the
lady's,' the reporter ventured.

Miss Pinkerton subsided crossly while he turned to
George.

'Was the object attached to anything? No wires or
anything? I mean, someone couldn't have been having
a joke or something?'

George gave a decent moment to the possibility.

'No,' he then said. 'It struck me, in fact, that there
was some sort of Mind behind it, operating from outer
space. It tried to attack me, in fact.'

'Really, how was that?'

'Mr. Lake was not attacked,' Miss Pinkerton stated.
'There was no danger at all. I saw the expression on
the pilot's face. He was having a game with Mr. Lake,
grinning all over his face.'

'Pilot?' said George. 'What are you talking about
— pilot!'

Miss Pinkerton sighed. 'A tiny man half the size of
my finger,' she declared. 'He sat on a tiny stool. He
held the little tiny steering-wheel with one hand and
waved with the other. Because, there was something
like a sewing-machine fixed near the rim, and he worked
the tiny treadle with his foot. Mr. Lake was not
attacked.'

'Don't be so damn silly,' said George.

'You don't mean this?' the reporter asked her with
scrutiny.

'Of course I do.'

'I would like to know something,' George demanded.

'You only saw the under side of the saucer, George.'

'You said nothing about any pilot at the time,' said George. 'I saw no pilot.'

'Mr. Lake got a fright when the saucer came at him. If he hadn't been dodging he would have seen for himself.'

'You mentioned no pilot,' said George. 'Be reasonable.'

'I had no chance,' said she. She appealed to the camera-man. 'You see, I know what I'm talking about. Mr. Lake thought he knew better, however. Mr. Lake said, "It's a forgery." If there's one thing I do know, it's china.'

'It would be most unlikely,' said George to the reporter. 'A steering-wheel and a treadle machine these days, can you credit it?'

'The man would have fallen out,' the camera-man reflected.

'I must say,' said the reporter, 'that I favour Mr. Lake's long-range theory. The lady may have been subject to some hallucination, after the shock of the saucer.'

'Quite,' said George. He whispered something to the photographer. 'Women!' Miss Pinkerton heard him breathe.

The reporter heard him also. He gave a friendly laugh. 'Shall we continue with Mr. Lake's account, and then see what we can make of both stories?'

But Miss Pinkerton had come to a rapid decision. She began to display a mood hitherto unknown to George. Leaning back, she gave way to a weak and artless giggling. Her hand fluttered prettily as she spoke between gurgles of mirth. 'Oh, what a mess! What an evening! We aren't accustomed to drink, you see, and now oh dear, oh dear!'

'Are you all right, Laura?' George enquired severely.

'Yes, yes, yes,' said Miss Pinkerton, drowsy and amiable. 'We really oughtn't have done this, George. Bringing these gentlemen out. But I can't keep it up, George. Oh dear, it's been fun though.'

She was away into her giggles again. George looked bewildered. Then he looked suspicious.

'It's definitely the effect of this extraordinary phenomenon,' George said firmly to the Press.

'It was my fault, all my fault,' spluttered Miss Pinkerton.

The reporter looked at his watch. 'I can quite definitely say you saw a flying object?' he asked. 'And that you were both put out by it?'

'Put down that it was a small, round, flattish object. We both agree to that,' George said.

A spurt of delight arose from Miss Pinkerton again.

'Women, you know! It always comes down to women in the finish,' she told them. 'We had a couple of drinks.'

'Mr. Lake had rather more than I did,' she added triumphantly.

'I assure you,' said George to the reporter.

'We might be fined for bringing the Press along, George. It might be an offence,' she put in.

'I assure you,' George insisted to the photographer, 'that we had a flying saucer less than an hour ago in this room.'

Miss Pinkerton giggled.

The reporter looked round the room with new eyes; and with the air of one to whom to understand all is to forgive all, he folded his notebook. The camera-man stared at the pool of sherry, the overturned flowers, the broken glass and china. He packed up his camera, and they went away.

George gave out the tale to his regular customers. He gave both versions, appealing to their reason to choose. Further up the road at her corner shop, Miss Pinkerton smiled tolerantly when questioned. 'Flying saucer? George is very artistic,' she would say, 'and allowances must be made for imaginative folk.' Sometimes she added that the evening had been a memorable one, 'Quite a party!'

It caused a certain amount of tittering in the neighbourhood. George felt this; but otherwise, the affair made no difference between them. Personally, I believe the story, with a preference for Miss Pinkerton's original version. She is a neighbour of mine. I have reason to believe this version because, not long afterwards, I too received a flying visitation from a saucer. The little pilot, in my case, was shy and inquisitive. He pedalled with all his might. My saucer was Royal Worcester, fake or not I can't say.

' A Sad Tale's Best for Winter '

THERE was a man lived by a graveyard. His name
was Selwyn Macgregor, the nicest boy who ever
committed the sin of whisky.

'Selwyn, what a place to live!'

'Have a tot for the road, dear.'

'Oh, Selwyn!'

'I get my letter tomorrow. Tomorrow I get the
letter.'

'Now, Selwyn Macgregor!'

'It always arrives the first of the month. The first it
always comes.'

'Macgregor, you're a case. Make it a small one.'

'For the road, mind.'

'Mac, I'm on my way. What a place to live, what a
graveyard and the mucky old church with the barbed
wire round it, who'd ever want to trespass within
yon?'

'Cheerio, cheers!'

'Here's to you, Mr. Macgregor. I would have to be
a sore old tramp to shelter in yon for the night. The
barbed wire I cannot understand, I can not.'

'The money comes on the first.'

'I'm away, Selwyn, the night's begun to rise.'

So it continued for thirteen years, with Selwyn
increasing in age from twenty-five to thirty-eight. At

twenty-five he was invalided out of the army, at thirty-eight was still living in the shack in the garden of the fallen manse. There by the graveyard he was still getting his letter from Edinburgh every month on the first, when he would cash the cheque.

'Good evening, Mr. Macgregor.'

'Just a tot, the both of you, come on now.'

'Mr. Macgregor, we beg to enquire, will you play the piano at the concert?'

'Aw, but that's to be the middle of the month.'

'Mac, you will play us a piece.'

'Mid-month I'll be in contemplation.'

'No more for me — well, a small . . . that's enough, Mr. M.'

'Cheerio!'

'We'll put you down for a tune then, Selwyn.'

'Aw no,' I said.

'Mr. Selwyn, you'll go melancholy mad. What a place to dwell by!'

'Here's luck t'you both.'

Always, about the middle of the month, Selwyn's money ran dry. Then he would go thirsty; he wouldn't open the door to anyone even if they had a plate of dinner in their hands. He lived on what he could get, turnips and sometimes the loaves and dinners which they left on the doorstep. The 25th of the month he opened his doors again, borrowed a bit till the first, received visitors, brought out the bottle.

But in those ten silent days between the middle of the month and the twenty-fifth Selwyn Macgregor would sit by his window and contemplate the graves of the dead.

Selwyn's aunt lived in a tenement flat in the War-render district of Edinburgh. Those flats were once occupied by people of good substance and still here and there contain a whole lot of wealth behind the lack of show.

'The district's going down,' Selwyn's aunt was saying for twenty years. But let anyone come and tell her, 'This quarter's going down':

'Not in my consideration, it isn't,' she would say.

It was Selwyn's Aunt Macgregor who, in view of the fact that his mother had been Welsh, sent him his monthly cheque, for it wasn't Selwyn's fault that his mother had been Welsh and mad or at least bone lazy. What's bred in the bone comes out.

There wouldn't be much point in going into many details about Aunt Macgregor, what she looked like in her navy blue and how her eyes, nose and mouth were disposed among the broken veins of her fine severe old face, because her features went, as Selwyn said, under the earth where corruption is, and her navy blue went to the nurse.

Well, she died. Some months before, you must know, she visited Selwyn up there in that shack by the grave-yard. She wore her brown, for she was careful with the navy. So up she went on the excursion to Selwyn Macgregor. He wasn't contemplating just then, so the doors were open.

'Auntie Macgregor! A little drop, Auntie, oh come on, a bit of a drop. That's the girl.'

'Selwyn,' she said, 'you're the worse.'

'Worse than what?' Although Selwyn knew she meant for the drink.

'Worse than what? Worse than who? Than who-oo-ooo?' Selwyn kept on chanting, and she started to laugh. She had a soft spot really for Selwyn.

Well, she died and left him a packet. Selwyn travelled to the funeral, a bitter cold day. Bitter cold, and naturally he had his flask in his pocket. For you must know Selwyn entertained a lively faith in the Resurrection; work it out, there was no dishonour meant to Aunt Macgregor by Selwyn's taking precautions against the cold at the graveside, though he tottered and there was talk.

'Dust to dust . . .'

'That's never Miss Macgregor's nephew! Surely yon's never!'

'That's the chief mourner, her brother's boy. What's he up to for the Lord's sake?'

Selwyn lifted a handful of earth. But then, then, he stood looking at it with his smile. There was the coffin waiting and all the people waiting. So when the minister nodded as if to say, 'All right, toss it on the coffin,' Selwyn flung the earth over his left shoulder out of force of habit, as he did at home with the salt. After that he beamed round at the mourners as much as to say, 'Here's health!' or 'Cheerio!' or some similar saying.

'Poor Miss Macgregor. The only relative, poor soul.'

.   .   .   .   .

Shortly afterwards Selwyn received a letter about his aunt's will from one of the trustees. It was rather complicated, and so Selwyn wrote, 'Come and see me after the twenty-fifth.' And he busied himself with contemplation until that date. On the twenty-sixth the trustee arrived at Selwyn's door with his healthy face and dark overcoat. Selwyn thought, what a nice wee trustee, here's hoping he's brought some ready.

'Make yourself at home,' said Selwyn, getting out another glass.

'Ta,' said the man.

'Here's hoping,' Selwyn said.

And eventually this trustee said to Selwyn, 'You know the provision in Miss Macgregor's will?'

'I did notice something,' Selwyn declared, 'in that letter you sent me but I was busy at the time.'

So the man read out the will, and when he came to the bit '. . . to my nephew Selwyn Macgregor . . .' he stopped and looked at Selwyn, '. . . providing,' he continued, 'he looks after his health.'

'My auntie all over,' Selwyn said and filled up the glasses. 'A very fine woman, Mr.———?'

'Brown,' said the man. 'My partner Mr. Harper is the other trustee. You'll get on fine with him. When will you be moving from here?'

'Aw when I'm dead,' said Selwyn.

'Now, Mr. Macgregor, this is not a healthy spot. The will says———'

'To hell with the will,' said Selwyn, and patted Mr. Brown on the shoulder, so that Mr. Brown couldn't help warming to him, what with the whisky-tingle inside him, and the pleasant Welsh lilt of the 'l's' when Selwyn had said, 'To hell with the will.'

'My work keeps me here,' Selwyn added.

'What is your work, Mr. Macgregor?'

'The contemplation of corruption.'

'Now, Mr. Macgregor, that is not a healthy occupation. I don't wish to be difficult but my partner Mr.

Harper takes his duty as a trustee very much to heart. Miss Macgregor was an old client of ours and she always worried about your health.'

'Bung ho, press on!' said Selwyn.

'Same to you, Mr. Mac. Here's to you, sir.'

'You can tell Harper,' Selwyn pointed out, 'that you found me in good health and busy working.'

'You look a bit thin, Mr. Macgregor. This doesn't look a healthy spot to me.'

Selwyn played him a tune and sang him a song. 'O mother, mother,' he sang, 'make my bed. O make it soft and narrow . . .'

'Very nice,' said the trustee when he'd finished. 'That was rare.'

'I'm a musician,' said Selwyn. 'You needn't mention my other work to Harper.'

'Here, you're trying to corrupt me, that'll never do. Didn't you say corruption was your line?'

'No, no. I do contemplation of corruption,' Selwyn explained. 'A very different thing, very high. Drink up.'

'Here's wishing you all you wish yourself,' said Mr. Brown. 'You don't corrupt me, mind!'

'It's either I corrupt you or you corrupt me,' Selwyn stated, and he went on to explain himself, and they argued the point while the time became timeless and they got muddled over the word corrupt, calling it cupped.

'Who's cupping who?' said Mr. Brown. 'Who's cups?'

Eventually Selwyn couldn't laugh for coughing, and again, he couldn't cough for laughing. When he recovered he passed the bottle and went deep

71

into the question of cups being a corrupt form of corrupt.

He sang out, 'Ha, ha, ha. Hee, hee, hee. I'll cup you or you'll cup me.'

'Here's a short life and a merry one!' said Mr. Brown.

. . . . . .

Well, it was Selwyn corrupted the trustee. His monthly cheque, bigger than before, continued to come in. All through the winter he carried on his routine, doors open for company on the twenty-fifth, and on the fifteenth doors shut, and Selwyn at his window contemplating the dead graves.

He died the following spring. There had been an X-ray two years back, when Selwyn had said, 'Aw to hell with my chest, I've work to do. Here's a health!'

Mr. Brown said to his partner, 'He never told me of his chest. If I'd known of it I would have seen him into a warm house and a new suit. I would have seen him with a housekeeper and I would have seen him into medical hands.'

'These musicians,' said Mr. Harper. 'Too dedicated. One must admire them, though.'

'Oh, must one? Oh, must one?' said Mr. Brown irritably, for he couldn't himself think highly of Selwyn who had been so shabby as to actually die when he had more or less agreed only to contemplate.

'A sad tale,' said Mr. Harper dreamily. 'Macgregor was a hero in his way.'

'Oh, was he? Oh, was he?' At that moment Mr. Brown despised his stupid partner almost more than he resented the dead man. Though lately, chancing to be in those parts where Selwyn had lived, even Mr. Brown couldn't help the thought, 'Oh, Selwyn Macgregor, what a manner you had!' And when he saw that they had levelled out the old graveyard to make a playground for the children, he contemplated Selwyn's corruption for a long time.

The Go-Away Bird

I

ALL over the Colony it was possible to hear the subtle voice of the grey-crested lourie, commonly known as the go-away bird by its call, 'go'way, go'way.' It was possible to hear the bird, but very few did, for it was part of the background to everything, a choir of birds and beasts, the crackle of vegetation in the great prevalent sunlight, and the soft rhythmic pad of natives, as they went barefoot and in single-file, from kraal to kraal.

Out shooting with her uncle and her young friends, happy under her wide-brimmed hat, Daphne du Toit would sometimes hear the go-away bird. Sometimes, during the school holidays, her aunt and uncle would have the young neighbours over from farms thirty miles distant. They would scrounge a lift into the nearest township — 'the dorp' they called it, for it was no more than a sandy main street in a valley, frequently cut off in the rainy season, when the rivers would swell above the bridges.

As they rumbled down the hill in the Ford V8 the uneven line of corrugated iron roofs would rise to meet them, and presently the car would stop outside the post office which was also the headquarters of the Native Commissioner. They would spill out to receive calls and glances of recognition from the white population. Natives would appear from nowhere to group themselves a few yards from the car, grinning with a kind of interest. They would amble past the general European store, two or three native stores and a dozen haphazard houses with voices of women scolding their servants rising from behind the torn mosquito-wire around the dark stoeps. Though it was a British colony, most of the people who lived in the dorp and its vicinity were Afrikaans, or Dutch as they were simply called. Daphne's father had been Dutch, but her mother had been a Patterson from England, and since their death she had lived with her mother's relations, the Chakata Pattersons, who understood, but preferred not to speak Afrikaans. Chakata was sixty, he had been very much older than Daphne's mother, and his own children were married, were farming in other colonies. Chakata nourished a passionate love for the natives. No-one had called him James for thirty-odd years; he went by the natives' name for him, Chakata. He loved the natives as much as he hated the Dutch.

Daphne had come into his household when she was six, both parents then being dead. That year Chakata was awarded an O.B.E. for his model native villages. Daphne remembered the great creaky motor vans and horse-drawn, sometimes ox-drawn, covered wagons pouring into the farm from far distances, thirty miles or five hundred miles away, neighbours come to congratulate Chakata. The empty bottles piled up in the yard. The native boys ran about all day to attend to the guests, some of whom slept in the house, most of whom bedded down in their wagons. Some were Dutch, and these, when they dismounted from their wagons, would kneel to thank God for a safe arrival. They would

75

then shout their orders to their servants and go to greet Old Tuys who had come out to welcome them. Chakata always fell back a little behind Old Tuys when Dutch visitors came to the farm. This was out of courtesy and tact for Old Tuys, the tobacco manager on Chakata's farm who was Dutch, and Chakata felt that these Afrikaanders would want to linger first with him, and exchange something sociable in Afrikaans. As for Chakata, although he spoke at least twenty native dialects, he would no more think of speaking Afrikaans than he would think of speaking French. The Dutch visitors would have to congratulate Chakata on his O.B.E. in the English tongue, however poorly managed, if they really wished to show they meant him well. Everyone knew that Old Tuys was a constant irritant to Chakata, addressing him usually in Dutch, to which Chakata invariably replied in English.

During those weeks following Chakata's return from Government House with the Order, when he kept open-house, Daphne would loiter around the farmhouse, waiting for the arrival of the cars and wagons, in the hope that they might bring a child for her to play with. Her only playmate was the cook's piccanin, Moses, a year older than Daphne, but frequently he was called away to draw water, sweep the yard, or fetch wood. He would trot across the yard with a pile of wood pressed against his chest and rising up to his eyes, clutching it officiously in his black arms which themselves resembled the faggots he bore. When Daphne scampered after Moses to the well or the wood-pile one of the older natives would interfere. 'No, Missy Daphne, you no do piccanin's work. You go make play.' She would wander off barefoot to the paddock beyond the guava bushes, or to the verging plantation of oranges, anywhere except the tobacco sheds, for there she might bump into Old Tuys who would then stop what he was doing, stand straight and, folding his arms, look at her with his blue eyes and sandy face. She would stare at him for a frightened moment and then run for it.

Once when she had been following a dry river-bed which cut through Chakata's land she nearly trod on a snake, and screaming, ran blindly to the nearest farm buildings, the tobacco sheds. Round the corner of one of the sheds came Old Tuys, and in her panic and relief at seeing a human face, Daphne ran up to him. 'A snake! There's a snake down the river-bed!' He straightened up, folded his arms, and looked at her until she turned and ran from him, too.

Old Tuys was not yet sixty. He had been called Young Tuys until his wife was known definitely to have committed adultery, not once, but a number of times. After her death it was at first a matter of some surprise among the farmers that Old Tuys did not leave Chakata's, for with his sound health and experience of tobacco, he could have been anyone's manager in or beyond the Colony. But word got round why Tuys remained with Chakata, and the subject was no more mentioned, save as passed on from fathers to sons, mothers to daughters, like the local genealogies, the infallible methods of shooting to kill, and the facts of life.

Daphne was only half conscious of the go-away bird, even while she heard it, during the first twelve years of her life. In fact she learnt about it at school during Natural History, and immediately recognised the fact

77

that she had been hearing this bird calling all her life.
She began to go out specially to hear it, and staring
into the dry river-bed, or brushing round the orange
trees, she would strain for its call; and sometimes at
sundowner time, drinking her lemonade between
Chakata and his wife on the stoep, she would say,
'Listen to the go-away bird.'

'No,' said Chakata one evening, 'it's too late. They
aren't about as late as this.'

'It *was* the Bird,' she said, for it had assumed for
her sufficient importance to be called simply this, like
the biblical Dove, or the zodiacal Ram.

'Look yere, Daphne, ma girl,' said Mrs. Chakata,
between two loud sucks of whisky and water, 'chuck
up this conversation about the blerry bird. If that's
all they teach you at the blerry boarding-school——'

'It's Natural History,' Chakata put in. 'It's a very
good thing that she's interested in the wild life around us.'

Mrs. Chakata had been born in the Colony. She
spoke English with the African Dutch accent, although
her extraction was English. Some said, however, that
there was a touch of colour, but this was not sufficiently
proved by her crinkled brown skin: many women in
the Colony were shrivelled in complexion, though they
were never hatless, nor for long in the sun. It was
partly the dry atmosphere of the long hot season and
partly the continual whisky drinking that dried most
of them up. Mrs. Chakata spent nearly all day in
her kimono dressing-gown lying on the bed, smoking
to ease the pains in her limbs the nature of which no
doctor had yet been able to diagnose over a period of
six years.

Since ever Daphne could remember, when Mrs.

Chakata lay on her bed in the daytime she had a revolver on a table by her side. And sometimes, when Chakata had to spend days and nights away from the farm, Daphne had slept in Mrs. Chakata's room, while outside the bedroom door, on a makeshift pallet, lay Ticky Talbot, the freckled Englishman who trained Chakata's racers. He lay with a gun by his side, treating it all as rather a joke.

From time to time Daphne had enquired the reasons for these precautions. 'You can't trust the munts,' said Mrs. Chakata, using the local word for the natives. Daphne never understood this, for Chakata's men were the finest in the Colony, that was an axiom. She vaguely thought it must be a surviving custom of general practice, dating from the Pioneer days, when white men and women were frequently murdered in their beds. This was within living history, and tales of these past massacres and retributions were part of daily life in the great rural districts of the Colony. But the old warrior chiefs were long-since dead, and the warriors disbanded, all differences now being settled by the Native Commissioners. As she grew older Daphne thought Mrs. Chakata and her kind very foolish to take such elaborate precautions against something so remote as a native rising on the farm. But it was not until the Coates family moved in to the neighbouring farm thirty-five miles away that Daphne discovered Mrs. Chakata's precautionary habits were not generally shared by the grown-up females of the Colony. Daphne was twelve when the Coates family, which included two younger girls and two older boys, came to the district. During the first school holidays after their arrival she was invited over to stay with them. Mr.

Coates had gone on safari, leaving his wife and children on the farm. The only other European there was a young married student of agriculture who lived on their land two miles from the farmhouse.

Daphne was put up on a camp bed in Mrs. Coates's bedroom. She noticed that her hostess had no revolver by her side, nor was anyone on sentry duty outside the door.

'Aren't you afraid of the muntus?' said Daphne.

'Good gracious, why? Our boys are marvellous.'

'Auntie Chakata always sleeps with a pistol by her side.'

'Is she afraid of rape, then?' said Mrs. Coates. All the children in the Colony understood the term; rape was a capital offence, and on very remote occasions the Colony would be astir about a case of rape, whether the accused was a white man or a black.

It was a new thought to Daphne that Mrs. Chakata might fear rape, not murder as she had supposed. She looked at Mrs. Coates with wonder. 'There isn't anyone, is there, would rape Auntie Chakata?' Mrs. Coates was smiling to herself.

Often, when she was out with the Coates children, Daphne would hear the go-away bird. One day when the children were walking through a field of maize, the older Coates boy, John, said to Daphne,

'Why do you suddenly stop still like that?'

'I'm listening to the go-away bird,' she said.

Her face was shaded under the wide brim of her hat, and the maize rose all round her, taller than herself. John Coates, who was sixteen, folded his arms and looked at her, for it was an odd thing for a little girl to notice the go-away bird.

'What are you looking at?' she said.

He didn't answer. The maize reached to his shoulder. He was put into a dither, and so he continued to look at her, arms folded, as if he felt confident.

'Don't stand like that,' Daphne said. 'You remind me of Old Tuys.'

John immediately laughed. He took his opportunity to gain a point, to alleviate his awkwardness and support his pose. 'You got a handful there with Old Tuys,' he said.

'Old Tuys is the best tobacco baas in the country,' she said defiantly. 'Uncle Chakata likes Old Tuys.'

'No, he does not like him,' said John.

'Yes, he does so, or he wouldn't keep him on.'

'My girl,' said John, '*I* know why Chakata keeps on Old Tuys. *You* know. Everyone knows. It isn't because he likes him.'

They moved on to join the other children. Daphne wondered why Chakata kept on Old Tuys.

They scrounged a lift to the dorp. The Coates family were uninhibited about speaking Afrikaans, chatting in rapid gutturals to people they met while Daphne stood by, shyly following what she could of the conversation.

They were to return to the car at five o'clock, and it was now only half-past three. Daphne took her chance and slipped away from the group through the post-office and out at the back yard where the natives were squatting round their mealie-pot. They watched her with their childish interest as she made her way past the native huts and the privies and out on the sanitary lane at the foot of the yard.

Daphne nipped across a field and up the steep track

81

of Donald Cloete's kopje. It bore this name, because Donald Cloete was the only person who lived on the hill, although there were several empty shacks surrounding his.

Donald Cloete had been to Cambridge. Indoors, he had two photographs on the wall. One was Donald in the cricket team, not easily recognisable behind his wide, curly moustache and among the other young men who looked so like him and stood in the same stiff, self-assured manner that Daphne had observed in pictures of the Pioneer heroes. The picture was dated 1898. Another group showed Donald in uniform among his comrades of the Royal Flying Corps. It was dated 1918, but Donald behind his moustache did not look much older than he appeared in the Cambridge picture.

Daphne looked round the open door and saw Donald seated in his dilapidated cane chair. His white shirt was stained with beetroot.

'Are you drunk, Donald', she enquired politely, 'or are you sober?'

Donald always told the truth. 'I'm sober,' he said. 'Come in.'

At fifty-six his appearance now had very little in common with the young Cambridge cricketer or the R.F.C. pilot. He had been in hundreds of jobs, had married and lost his wife to a younger and more energetic man. The past eight years had been the most settled in his life, for he was Town Clerk of the dorp, a job which made few demands on punctuality, industry, smartness of appearance, and concentration, which qualities Donald lacked. Sometimes when the Council held its monthly meeting, and

Donald happened to stagger in late and drunk, the Chairman would ask Donald to leave the meeting, and in his absence propose his dismissal. Sometimes they unanimously dismissed him and after the meeting he was informed of the decision. However, next day Donald would dress himself cleanly and call in to see the butcher with a yarn about the R.F.C.; he would call on the headmaster who had been to Cambridge some years later than Donald; and after doing a round of the Council members he would busy himself in the district, would ride for miles on his bicycle seeing that fences were up where they should be, and sign-posts which had fallen in the rains set upright and prominent. Within a week, Donald's dismissal would be ignored by everyone. He would relax then, and if he entered up a birth or a death during the week, it was a good week's work.

'Who brought you from the farm?' said Donald.

'Ticky Talbot,' said Daphne.

'Nice to see you,' said Donald. And he called to his servant for tea.

'Five more years and then I go to England,' said Daphne, for this was the usual subject between them, and she did not feel it right to come to the real purpose of her visit so soon.

'That will be the time,' said Donald. 'When you go to England, that will be the time.' And he told her all over again about the water meadows at Cam-bridge, the country pubs, the hedging and ditching, the pink-coated riders.

Donald's ragged native brought in tea in two big cups, holding one in each hand. One he gave to Daphne and the other to Donald.

How small, Donald said, were the English streams which never dried up. How small the fields, little bits of acreage, and none of the cottage women bitchy for they did their own housework and had no time to bitch. And then, of course, the better classes taking tea in their long galleries throughout the land, in springtime, with the pale sunlight dripping through the mullioned windows on to the mellow Old Windsor chairs, and the smell of hyacinths. . . .

'Oh, I see. Now tell me about London, Donald. Tell me about the theatres and bioscopes.'

'They don't say "bioscope" there, they say "cinema" or "the pictures".'

'I say, Donald,' she said, for she noticed it was twenty-past four, 'I want you to tell me something straight.'

'Fire ahead,' said Donald.

'Why does Uncle Chakata keep on Old Tuys?'

'I don't want to lose my job,' he said.

'Upon my honour,' she said, 'if you tell me about Old Tuys I shan't betray you.'

'The whole Colony knows the story,' said Donald, 'but the first one to tell it to you is bound to come up against Chakata.'

'May I drop dead on this floor,' she said, 'if I tell my Uncle Chakata on you.'

'How old are you, now?' Donald said.

'Nearly thirteen.'

'It was two years before you were born — that would make it fifteen years ago, when Old Tuys . . .'

Old Tuys had already been married for some time to a Dutch girl from Pretoria. Long before he took the job at Chakata's he knew of her infidelities. They had one peculiarity: her taste was exclusively for Englishmen. The young English settlers whom she met in the various establishments where Tuys was employed were, guilty or not, invariably accosted by Tuys: 'You committed adultery with my wife, you swine.' There might be a fight, or Tuys would threaten his gun. However it might be, and whether or not these young men were his wife's lovers, Tuys was usually turned off the job.

It was said he was going to shoot his wife and arrange it to look like an accident. Simply because this intention was widely reported, he could not have carried out the plan successfully, even if he did, in fact, contemplate the deed. Certainly he beat her up from time to time.

Tuys hoped eventually to get a farm of his own. Chakata, who knew of his troubles, took Tuys on to learn the tobacco sheds. Tuys and his wife moved into a small house on Chakata's land. 'Any trouble with the lady, Tuys,' said Chakata, 'come to me, for in a young country like this, with four white men to every one white woman, there is bound to be trouble.'

There was trouble the first week with a trooper.

'Look here, Tuys,' said Chakata, 'I'll talk to her.' He had frequently in his life had the painful duty of giving his servants a talking-to on sex. At the Pattersons' home in England it had been a routine affair.

Hatty Tuys was not beautiful: in fact she was dark and scraggy. However, Chakata not only failed to reform her, he succumbed to her. She wept. She said she hated Tuys.

Donald paused in his story to remark to Daphne, 'Mind you, this sort of thing doesn't happen in England.'

85

'Doesn't it?' said Daphne.

'Oh well, there are love affairs but they take time. You have to sort of build them up with a woman. In England, a man of Chakata's importance might feel sorry for a slut if she started to cry, but he wouldn't just make love to her on the spot. The climate's cooler there, you see, and there are a lot more girls.'

'Oh, I see,' said Daphne. 'What did Uncle Chakata do next?'

'Well, as soon as he had played the fool with Mrs. Tuys he felt sorry. He told her it was a moment of weakness and it would never occur again. But it did.'

'Did Tuys find out?'

'Tuys found out. He went to Mrs. Chakata and tried to rape her.'

'Didn't it come off?'

'No, it didn't come off.'

'It must have been the whisky in her breath. It must have put him off,' said Daphne.

'In England,' said Donald, 'girls your age don't know very much about these things.'

'Oh, I see,' said Daphne.

'It's all different there. Well, Mrs. Chakata complained to Chakata, and wanted him to shoot Tuys. He refused, of course, and he gave Tuys a rise and made him manager. And from that day he wouldn't look at Mrs. Tuys, wouldn't even look at her. Whenever he caught sight of her about the farm, he looked the other way. In the end she wrote to Chakata to say she was mad in love with him and if she couldn't have him she would shoot herself. The note was written in block letters, in Afrikaans.'

'Chakata would never answer it, then,' Daphne said.

86

'You are right,' said Donald. 'And Mrs. Tuys shot herself. Old Tuys has sworn to be revenged on Chakata some day. That's why Mrs. Chakata has a gun at her bedside. She has implored Chakata to get rid of Old Tuys. So he should, of course.'

'He can't, very well, when you think of it,' said Daphne.

'It's only his remorse,' said Donald, 'and his English honour. If Old Tuys was an Englishman, Daphne, he would have cleared off the farm long ago. But no, he remains, he has sworn on the Bible to be revenged.'

'It must be our climate,' said Daphne. 'I have never liked the way Old Tuys looks at me.'

'The Colony is a savage place,' he said. He rose and poured himself a whisky. 'I grant you,' he said, 'we have the natives under control. I grant you we have the leopards under control——'

'Oh, remember Moses,' said Daphne. Her former playmate, Moses, had been got by a leopard two years ago.

'That was exceptional. We are getting control over malaria. But we haven't got *the savage in ourselves* under control. This place brings out *the savage in ourselves.*' He finished his drink and poured another. 'If you go to England,' he said, 'don't come back.'

'Oh, I see,' said Daphne.

She was ten minutes late when she arrived at the car. The party had been anxious about her.

'Where did you get to? You slipped away . . . we asked everywhere . . .'

John Coates said in a mock-girlish tone, 'Oh, she's been listening to the go-away bird out on the lone wide veldt.'

'Five more years and then I go to England. Four years . . . three . . .'

Meanwhile, life in the Colony seemed to become more exciting every year. In fact, it went on as usual, but Daphne's capacity for excitement developed as she grew into her teens.

She had a trip to Kenya to stay with a married cousin, another trip to Johannesburg with Mrs. Coates to buy clothes.

'Typical English beauty Daphne's turning out to be,' said Chakata. In reality she was too blonde to be typically English; she took after her father's family, the Cape du Toits who were a mixture of Dutch and Huguenot stock.

At sixteen she passed her matric and her name was entered for a teachers' training college in the Capital. During the holidays she flirted with John Coates who would drive her round the countryside in the little German Volkswagen which his father had obtained for him. They would go on Sunday afternoons to the Williams Hotel on the great main road for tea and a swim in the bathing-pool with all the district who converged there weekly from farms and towns.

'In England,' Daphne would tell him, 'you can bathe in the rivers. No bilharzia there, no crocs.'

'There's going to be a war in Europe,' said John.

Daphne would sit on the hotel stoep in her smart new linen slacks, sipping her gin and lime, delighted and amazed to be grown-up, to be greeted by her farming neighbours.

''Lo, Daphne, how are your mealies?'

'Not too bad, how are yours?'

'Hallo, Daphne, how's the tobacco?'

'Rotten, Old Tuys says.'

'I hear Chakata's sold La Flèche.'

'Well, he's had an offer, actually.'

She had been twice to a dance at Williams Hotel. Young Billy Williams who was studying medicine at Capetown proposed marriage to her, but as everyone knew, she was to go to college in the Capital and then to England to stay with the English Pattersons for a couple of years before she could decide about marriage.

War broke out at the beginning of her first term at the training college. All her old young men, as well as her new, became important and interesting in their uniforms and brief appearances on leave.

She took up golf. Sometimes, after a hole, when she was following her companions to the next tee, she would lag behind or even stop in her tracks.

'Feeling all right, Daphne?'

'Oh, I was only listening to the go-away bird.'

'Interested in ornithology?'

'Oh yes, fairly, you know.'

When she returned to the farm after her first term at the college Chakata gave her a revolver.

'Keep it beside your bed,' he said.

She took it without comment.

Next day, he said, 'Where did you go yesterday afternoon?'

'Oh, for a trek across the veldt, you know.'

'Anywhere special?'

'Only to Makata's kraal. He's quite determined to hang on to that land the Beresfords are after. He's got a wife for his son, he paid five head.' Makata was the local chief. Daphne enjoyed squatting in the shade of his great mud hut drinking the tea specially prepared for her, and though the rest of the Colony looked with disfavour on such visits, it was something which Chakata and his children had always done, and no-one felt inclined to take up the question with Chakata. Chakata wasn't just anyone.

'I suppose,' said Chakata to Daphne, 'you always carry a gun?'

'Well, yesterday,' said Daphne, 'I didn't actually.'

'*Always*,' said Chakata, 'take a gun when you go out on the veldt. It's a golden rule. There's nothing more exasperating than to see a buck dancing about in the bush and to find yourself standing like a fool without a gun.'

Since she was eight and had first learnt to shoot, this had been a golden rule of Chakata's. Many a time she had been out on her own, weighed down with the gun, and had seen dozens of buck and simply had not bothered to shoot. She hated venison, in any case. Tinned salmon was her favourite dish.

He seemed to know her thoughts. 'We're always short of buck for the dogs. Remember there's a war on. Remember *always*,' said Chakata, 'to take a gun. I hear on the wireless,' he added, 'that there's a leopard over in the Temwe valley. The mate has young. It's got two men, so far.'

'Uncle Chakata, that's a long way off,' Daphne said explosively.

'Leopards can travel,' said Chakata. He looked horribly put out.

'Oh, I see,' said Daphne.

'And you ought to ride more,' he said, 'it's far better exercise than walking.'

She saw that he was not really afraid of her meeting the leopard, nor did he need meat for the dogs; and she thought of how, yesterday afternoon, she had been followed all the way to the kraal by Old Tuys. He had kept to the bush, and seemed not to know he had been observed. She had been glad that several parties of natives had passed her on the way. Afterwards, when she was taking leave of Makata, he had offered to send his nephew to accompany her home. This was a customary offer: she usually declined it. This time, however, she had accepted the escort, who plodded along behind her until she dismissed him at the edge of the farm. Daphne did not mention this incident to Chakata.

That afternoon when she set off for tea at the Mission, she was armed.

Next day Chakata gave her the old Mercedes for herself. 'You walk too much,' he said.

It was no use now, checking off the years before she should go to England. She climbed Donald Cloete's kopje: 'Are you sober, Donald, or——?'

'I'm drunk, go away.'

Towards the end of her course at the training college, when she was home for the Christmas holidays, she rode her horse along the main wide road to the dorp. She did some shopping; she stopped to talk to the Cypriot tailor who supplied the district with drill shorts, and to the Sephardic Jew who kept the largest kaffir store.

'Live and let live,' said Chakata. But these people were never at the farm, and this was Daphne's only chance of telling them of her college life.

She called in at the Indian laundry to leave a bottle

of hair oil which, for some unfathomable reason, Chakata had promised to give to the Indian.

She had tea with the chemist's wife, then returned to the police station where she had left the horse. Here she stopped for about an hour chatting with two troopers whom she had known since her childhood. It was late when she set off up the steep main road, keeping well to the side of the tarmac strips on which an occasional car would pass, or a native on a bicycle. She knew all the occupants of the cars, and as they slowed down to pass her they would call a greeting. She had gone about five miles when she came to a winding section of the road with dense bush on either side. This part was notorious for accidents. The light was failing rapidly, and as she heard a car approaching round the bend ahead of her she reined in to the side. Immediately the car appeared its lights were switched on, but before they dazzled her she had recognised Old Tuys at the wheel of the shooting-brake. As he approached he gave no sign of slowing down. Not only did Old Tuys keep up his speed, he brought the car off the strips and passed within a few inches of the animal.

Daphne had once heard a trooper say that for a human being to fall in the bush at sundown or after was like a naked man appearing in class at a girl's school. As she landed in the dark thicket every living thing screeched, rustled, fled and flapped in a feminine sort of panic. The horse was away along the road, its hooves beating frantic diminishing signals in the dusk. Daphne's right shin was giving her intense pain. She was fairly sure Old Tuys had stopped the car. She rose and limped a few steps, pushing her way through the vegetation and branches, to the verge of the road. Here she stopped, for she heard footsteps on the road a few feet away. Old Tuys was waiting for her. She looked round her and quickly saw there was no chance of penetrating further into the bush with safety. The sky was nearly dark now, and the pain in her leg was threatening to overcome her. Daphne had never fainted, even when, once, she had wanted to, during an emergency operation for a snake-bite, the sharp blade cutting into her unanaesthetized flesh. Now, it seemed that she would faint, and this alarmed her, for she could hear Old Tuys among the crackling branches at the side of the road, and presently could discern his outline. The sound of a native shouting farther up the road intruded upon her desire to faint, and, to resist closing her eyes in oblivion she opened them wide, wider, staring into the darkness.

Old Tuys got hold of her. He did not speak, but he gripped her arm and dragged her out of the bush and threw her on the ground at the side of the road out of the glare of the headlamps. Daphne screamed and kicked out with her good leg. Old Tuys stood up, listening. A horse was approaching. Suddenly round the bend came a native leading Daphne's horse. It shied at the sight of the van's headlights, but the native held it firmly while Old Tuys went to take it.

'Clear off,' said Tuys to the boy in kitchen kaffir.

'Don't go,' shouted Daphne. The native stood where he was.

'I'll get you home in the van,' said Old Tuys. He bent to lift Daphne. She screamed. The native came and stood a little closer.

Daphne lifted herself to her feet. She was hysterical.

93

'Knock him down,' she ordered the native. He did not move. She realised he would not touch Old Tuys. The Europeans had a name of sticking together, and, whatever the circumstances, to hit a white man would probably lead to prison. However, the native was evidently prepared to wait, and when Old Tuys swore at him and ordered him off, he merely moved a few feet away.

'Get into the van,' shouted Tuys to Daphne. 'You been hurt in an accident. I got to take you home.'

A car came round the bend, and seeing the group by the standing car, stopped. It was Mr. Parker the headmaster.

Old Tuys started the tale about the accident, but Mr. Parker was listening to Daphne who limped across to him.

'Take me back to the farm, Mr. Parker, for God's sake.'

He helped her in and drove off. The native followed with the horse. Old Tuys got into the van and made off in the opposite direction.

'I won't go into details,' said Chakata to Daphne next day, 'but I can't dismiss Tuys. It goes back to an incident which occurred before you were born. I owe him a debt of honour. Something between men.'

'Oh, I see,' said Daphne.

Old Tuys had returned to the farm in the early hours of the morning. Daphne knew that Chakata had waited up for him. She had heard the indeterminate barking of a row between them.

She sat up in bed with her leg in splints.

'We could be raped and murdered,' said Mrs. Chakata, 'but Chakata still won't get rid of the bastard. Chakata would kick his backside out of it if he was a proper man.'

'He says it's because of a debt of honour,' said Daphne.

'That's all you get from Chakata. Whatever you do,' said Mrs. Chakata, 'don't marry a blerry Englishman. They got no thought for their wives and kids, they only got thought for their blerry honour.'

It had always been understood that she was to go to England in nineteen-forty, when she was eighteen. But now there was no question of going overseas till the war should end. Daphne had been to see a Colonel, a Judge and a Bishop: she wanted to go to England to join one of the women's services. They told her there was no hope of an exit permit for England being granted to a civilian. Besides, she was under age: would Chakata give his permission?

At twenty she took a teaching job in the Capital rather than join any of the women's services in the Colony, for these seemed to her feeble organisations compared with the real thing.

She was attracted by the vast new R.A.F. training camps which were being set up. One of them lay just outside the Capital, and most of her free time was spent at sundowners and dances in the mess, or weekend tennis parties at outlying farms where she met dozens of young fighter pilots with their Battle of Britain D.F.C.s. She was in love with them collectively. They were England. Her childhood neighbour, John Coates, was a pilot. He was drafted to England, but his ship and convoy were mined outside the Cape.

News of his death reached Daphne just after her twenty-first birthday.

She drove out to the camp with one of her new English friends to attend a memorial service for John at the R.A.F. chapel. On the way the tyre burst. The car came to a dangerous screeching stop five yards off the road. The young man set about changing the tyre. Daphne stood by.

He said to her for the third time, 'O.K. All *set*, Daphne.' She was craning her head absently.

'Oh,' she said, bringing her attention back to him. 'I was listening to the go-away bird.'

'What bird?'

'The grey-crested lourie. You can hear it all over the Colony. You hardly ever see it. It says "Go'way."'

He stood listening. 'I can't hear a thing.'

'It's stopped now,' she said.

'Are there any yellow-hammers here?' he said.

'No, I don't think so.'

'They say "a little bit of bread and *no* cheese",' he said.

'D'you find them all over England?'

'I think so. Anyway, there are millions in Hertfordshire.'

She engaged herself to marry a flight-lieutenant instructor. He was killed the following week in a flying accident. He had said, describing his home near Henley, 'Ghastly place really. The river simply walks over the garden. Father's been doubled with rheumatism, but won't move.' These words had somehow enchanted her. 'The river simply walks over the garden,' and she knew that the river was the Thames and that the garden was full of English bushes and all the year round was green. At his funeral she felt that the garden had gone under the sea. His family lived not far away from the English Pattersons. 'No,' he had said, 'I don't think we know them.' It seemed incredible that he did not know his neighbours of only fifteen miles distant. 'No,' wrote the English Pattersons, 'we don't know the people. Are they Londoners come down since the war? There are a lot of Londoners . . .'

In the Christmas holidays after her twenty-first birthday she said to Chakata, 'I'm giving a term's notice. I'm going to Capetown.'

'Have you had more trouble with Tuys?' he said.

'No. It's just that I want a change. I should like to see the sea.'

'Because, if you have had trouble with Tuys, I shall speak to him.'

'Are you at all thinking of getting rid of Old Tuys?' said Daphne.

'No,' he said.

He tried to persuade her to go to Durban instead of Capetown. 'Durban is more English.' He did not like the idea of her staying with her father's people, the du Toits, in Capetown.

Capetown made her hanker all the more for England. There was just enough of the European touch — old sedate Dutch houses, cottage gardens, green meadows, a symphony orchestra, a modern art gallery — to whet her appetite for the real thing. The fact that the servants were paler than those of the Colony and more European in feature, suggested to her a proximity to England where servants were white. 'We have no-one left,' wrote the English Pattersons, 'but Clara, and half the time *we* have to wait on *her*. She has lost her memory and she keeps thinking you are your mother. She thinks Toad is Uncle Pooh-bah. Aunt Sarah is a trial. *She* thinks we pinch her sweet coupons.'

Daphne longed to be waiting on Clara, to be accused by Aunt Sarah of stealing the coupons, to be washing up the dishes and climbing over stiles with the cousins whom she had never seen. Some of her relations were nicknamed after characters in *The Wind and the Willows*, Rat, Mole, Toad, others named from as yet unaccountable sources — her uncles Pooh-bah and The Dong, for instance. The du Toits could not quite follow the drift of Daphne's letters from England when she read them aloud, herself carried away by the poetry of the thing. 'Rat,' she would explain, 'is Henry Middleton, Molly's husband. He's in the navy. . . .'

'Doesn't he treat her right, then?'

'He adores her actually,' said Daphne, using the infectious phraseology of the letters from England.

'Why does she call him a rat, then?'

Chakata was right, thought Daphne, you simply can't explain the English sense of humour.

She went to night clubs in Capetown, keeping steadily in her thoughts the fact, of which she was convinced, that these were but tawdry versions of the London variety.

The du Toits were members of an Afrikaans élite. They tolerated but did not cultivate the English. One of their cousins, an Oxford graduate now fighting in North Africa, came home on leave and made a bid for Daphne. Just at that moment she became attached to a naval officer who had arrived a fortnight ago in a corvette which had been badly hit. Ronald was the most typical, Daphne thought, Englishman she had ever met, and the most unaffected. The ship, he whispered confidentially, for no-one was supposed to know it, would be in port for six weeks. Meanwhile, might they consider themselves engaged? Daphne said, oh really, all right. And regardless of anything the du Toits might speculate, she spent a night with him at a sea-front hotel. With the utmost indifference Ronald mentioned that, before the war, he had captained the village cricket team — 'The squire usually does.' Daphne saw, in a vision, numerous long white-flannelled legs, the shadowy elms, pretty sisters in pastel dresses, the mothers in old-fashioned florals and the fathers in boaters, all cool and mellow as the lemonade being served, under the marquee by the lake, on trays borne by pale-faced, black-frocked, white-frilled maids. Daphne thought of the heat and glare of Chakata's farm, the smell of the natives, and immediately felt bloated and gross.

A few days later, while she was dancing cheek-to-cheek with Ronald, at the tea-dance provided by the hotel on the sea-front, to the strains of

> *The fundamental things apply*
> *As time goes by*

— at the same moment young Jan du Toit was informing the assembled family that Daphne's fiancé was a married man.

Her aunt Sonji spoke to Daphne next morning.

Daphne said, 'He's the captain of his local cricket team.'

'He could still be a married man,' said Sonji.

By lunch-time the information was confirmed, and by sundown the corvette had sailed.

Daphne felt irrationally that it was just the sort of thing one would expect to happen while living with the du Toits. She removed to Durban, treating the English ships with rather more caution than hitherto. She eschewed altogether the American navy which had begun to put in frequent appearances.

Among her colleagues at the school where she taught in Durban was a middle-aged art master who had emigrated from Bristol some years before the war. He saw England as the Barbarian State which had condemned him to be an art master instead of an artist. He spoke often to Daphne on these sad lines, but she was not listening. Or rather, what she was listening to were the accidentals of this discourse. 'Take a fashionable portrait painter,' he would say. 'He is prepared to flatter his wealthy patrons — or more often patron*esses*. He's willing to turn 'em out pretty on the canvas. He can then afford to take a Queen Anne house in Kensington, Chelsea or Hampstead, somewhere like that. He turns the attic into a studio, a great window frontage. A man I know, was at college with me, he's a fashionable portrait painter now, has a studio overlooking the Regent's Canal, gives parties, goes everywhere, Henley, Ascot, titled people, dress designers, film people. That's the sort of successful artist England produces to-day.'

Daphne's mind played like the sun over the words 'Queen Anne house', 'Kensington', 'Chelsea', 'Studio', 'Regent's Canal', 'Henley'. She had ears for nothing else.

'Now take another fellow,' continued the art master, 'I knew at college. He hadn't much talent, rather ultra-modern, but he wanted to be an artist and he wouldn't be anything else. What has he got for it? The last time I saw him he hadn't the price of a tube of paint. He was sharing a Soho attic with another artist — who's since become famous as a theatrical designer incidentally — name G. T. Marvell. Heard of him?'

'No,' Daphne said.

'Well, he's famous now.'

'Oh, I see.'

'But the artist he was living with in Soho never got anywhere. They used to partition the room with blankets and clothes hung on a piece of rope. That's the sort of thing you get in Soho. The native in the bush is better off than the artist in England.'

Daphne took home all such speeches of discouragement, and pondered them with delight: 'Soho', 'poet', 'attic', 'artist'.

In 1946, at last, she got a place on a boat. She went to say good-bye to Chakata. She sat with the ageing man on the stoep.

'Why did *you* never go back to England for a visit?' she said.

'There has always been too much to do on the farm,' he said. 'I could never leave it.' But his head inclined towards the room at the back of the stoep, where Mrs. Chakata lay on her bed, the whisky and the revolver by her side. Daphne understood how Chakata, having made a mistake in marriage, could never have taken Mrs. Chakata home to the English Pattersons, nor could he ever have left her in the Colony, even with friends, for he was a man of honour.

'I suppose,' said Daphne, 'the Pattersons will be thrilled to hear about our life out here.'

He looked worried. 'Remember,' he said, 'that Auntie Chakata is an invalid. At home they don't understand tropical conditions, and——'

'Oh, I shall explain about Auntie Chakata,' she said, meaning she would hush it up.

'I know you will,' he said admiringly.

She walked over to Makata's kraal to say goodbye. There was a new Makata; the old chief was dead. The new chief had been educated at the Mission, he wore navy-blue shorts and a white shirt. Whereas old Makata used to speak of his tribe as 'the men', this one called them 'my people'. She had used to squat with old Makata on the ground outside his large rondavel. Now a grey army blanket was spread, on which two kitchen chairs were placed for the chief and his visitor. Daphne sat on her kitchen chair and remembered how strongly old Makata used to smell; it was the unwashed native smell. Young Makata smelt of carbolic soap. 'My people will pray for you,' he said. He did not offer to send a man to escort her to the farm, as old Makata had always done.

She knew Old Tuys had followed her to the kraal, and she was aware that he was awaiting her return. Her arms were swinging freely, but she had a small revolver in the pocket of her shorts.

A mile from the farm Old Tuys walked openly over the veldt towards her. He was carrying a gun. Daphne doubled as casually as possible into the bush. It was sparse at this point, and so she was easily visible. She picked her way through the low brushwood, moving towards the farm. She heard Old Tuys crackling through the dry wood behind her.

'Stop there,' she heard him say, 'or I shoot.'

Her hand was on her revolver, and it was her intention to wheel round and shoot before he could aim his gun. But as she turned she heard a shot from behind him and saw him fall. Daphne heard his assailant retreating in the bush behind him, and then on the veldt track the fading sound of bicycle wheels.

Old Tuys was still conscious. He had been hit in the base of the neck. Daphne looked down at him.

'I'll send them to fetch you,' she said.

The following week the police made half-hearted raids on the native dwellings in the district. No firearms were discovered. In any case, Daphne had called in at the police station, and told her old friend, Johnnie Ferreira, that if any man black *or* white was brought to trial for shooting Old Tuys, she would give evidence for the assailant.

'Old Tuys was after you, then?'

'He was. I had a revolver and I intended to use it. Only the other got him first.'

'Quite *sure* you didn't see who shot him?'

'No. Why?'

'Because you say "black or white". We have been more or less assuming it was a native since we understand the man had a bicycle.'

'Black or white,' said Daphne, 'it makes no difference. He was only doing his duty.'

'Oh, I know,' said Johnnie, 'but we like to know the facts. If we got the man, you see, there are good grounds for having the charge against him dismissed, then we should bring Old Tuys on a charge when he comes out of hospital. It's about time Chakata was rid of that slug.'

'Well, you haven't got the man,' said Daphne, 'have you?'

'No,' he said. 'But if you have any ideas, come and let's know. Think it over.'

Daphne parked the car at the foot of Donald Cloete's kopje and climbed slowly, stopping frequently to look at the wide land below, the little dorp, the winding main road, and faintly, the farm roofs in the distance. She took in the details like a camera, and as if for the first time, for soon she would be gone to England.

She sat on a stone. A lizard slid swiftly between her feet and disappeared among the grasses.

'Go'way. Go'way.'

The sound darted forth and vanished. Two or three times she had seen the go-away bird. It was quite colourless, insignificant. She rose and plodded on.

'D. or S., Donald?'

'So-so. Come in.'

'Johnnie Ferreira wants to bring a charge against Old Tuys,' she said, 'for his attempt on me the other day.'

'I know,' he said, 'Johnnie's boys have been here.'

'What did you say?'

'I told them to try elsewhere.'

There were few white men in the Colony who rode bicycles, and only one in the district. Bicycles were used mostly by natives and a few schoolboys. All the children were away at school. Daphne's unknown protector was therefore either a passing native or Donald doing his rounds. Moreover, there was the question of the gun. Few natives, if they owned firearms, would be likely to risk betraying this illicit fact. And few natives, however gallant, would risk the penalty for shooting a white man.

'Why not let them put Old Tuys on charge?' said Daphne.

'I don't prevent them,' he said. 'They can go ahead.'

'They need a witness,' she said. 'Otherwise it's his word against mine. Old Tuys would probably be acquitted on appeal.'

'Nothing doing,' he said. 'I don't like the law-courts.'

'Well, it *was* very nice of you, Donald,' she said. 'I'm grateful.'

'Then don't talk to me about law cases.'

'All right, I won't.'

'You see,' he said, 'how it is. Chakata wouldn't like the scandal. All the past might come out. You never know what might come out if they start questioning Old Tuys in the courts. Old Chakata wouldn't like it.'

'I think he knows what you did, Donald. He's very grateful.'

'He'd been more grateful if Old Tuys had been killed.'

'Did you catch Old Tuys on purpose or did you just happen to be there when Old Tuys came after me?' she enquired.

'Don't know what you mean. I was putting up the Foot and Mouth notices that day. I was busy. I've got more to do than keep Old Tuys in sight.'

'I'm going away next week,' she said, 'for about two years.'

'So I hear. You have no conception of the greenness of the fields. It rains quite often. . . . Go to see the Tower. . . . Don't return.'

II

Linda Patterson, aged twenty-eight, was highly discontented. Daphne could not see why. She herself adored Uncle Pooh-bah with his rheumatism and long woollen combies. Only his constant threats to sell the damp old house and go to live in some hotel alarmed Daphne at the same time as the idea gave hope to her cousin Linda. Linda's husband had been killed in a motor accident. She longed to be free to take a job in London.

'How could you leave that lovely climate and come to this dismal place?' Linda would say.

'But,' Daphne said happily, 'this at least is England.'

Not long after she arrived Aunt Sarah, who was eighty-two, said to Daphne, 'My dear, it isn't done.'

'What isn't done?'

Aunt Sarah sighed, 'You know very well what I mean. My nightdresses dear, the rayon ones. There were three in my drawer, a green, a peach and a pink. I only discovered this morning that they were gone. Now there is no-one else in this house who could have taken them but you. Clara is above reproach, and besides, she can't climb the stairs, how could she? Linda has lots of nighties left over from her trousseau, poor gel——'

'What are you saying?' said Daphne. 'What are you saying?'

Aunt Sarah took a pin out of her needle-box and pricked Daphne on the arm. 'That's for stealing my nighties,' she said.

'She'll have to go to a home,' said Linda. 'We can't

keep a daily woman for more than a week because of
Aunt Sarah's accusing them of stealing.'

Pooh-bah said, 'D'you know, apart from *that one thing*
she's quite normal, really. Wonderful for her age. If
we could only somehow get her to realise how utterly
foolish she is over *that one thing*——'

'She'll have to go to a home.'

Pooh-bah went out to look at the barometer and did
not return.

'I don't mind, really,' said Daphne.

'Look at the work she causes,' said Linda. 'Look at
the trouble!'

Next day, when Daphne was scrubbing the kitchen
floor Aunt Sarah came and stood in a puddle before
her. 'My Friars Balsam,' she said. 'I left a full bottle
in the bathroom, and it's gone.'

'I know,' said Daphne, scrubbing away, 'I took it in
a weak moment, but now I've put it back.'

'Very well,' said Aunt Sarah, trotting off and drag-
ging the puddle with her. 'But don't do it again.
Pilfering was always a great weakness in your mother,
I recall.'

The winter temperature lasted well into April.
Linda and Daphne had to sit by a one-bar electric fire
in the library if they wanted to smoke; Pooh-bah's
asthma was affected by cigarette smoke.

Linda was conducting a week-end liaison with a
barrister in London, and with Daphne in the house she
found it easier to disappear for longer week-ends, and
then, sometimes, a week. 'Daphne,' she would say on
the phone, 'you don't mind holding the fort, honestly?
This is so important to me.'

Daphne went for walks with Uncle Pooh-bah. She

had to take short steps, for he was slow. They walked on the well-laid paths to the river which Daphne always referred to as 'the Thames', which indeed, of course, it was.

'We went as far as the Thames,' Daphne would tell Linda on their return. They ventured no farther than the local lock, a walk bordered with green meadows and wonderful sheep.

Relations of some friends in the Colony invited her to London. She accepted, then told Linda when she would be away.

'But,' said Linda, '*I* shall be in London next week. It's important, you know. Someone's got to look after Pooh-bah and Aunt Sarah.'

'Oh, I see,' said Daphne.

Linda cheered up. 'Perhaps you could go the week after?'

'No, next week,' said Daphne patiently, 'that's when I'm going.'

'*Someone's* got to look after Pooh-bah and Aunt Sarah.'

'Oh, I see.'

Linda started to cry. Daphne said, 'I'll write to my friends, and explain.'

Linda dried her eyes and said, 'You can't imagine how deadly it is living in this awful house year after year with a couple of selfish old people and that helpless Clara.'

Next week-end, while Linda was away, several Patterson relations arrived. Molly, Rat, Mole and an infant called Pod. Mole was an unattached male cousin. Daphne expressed a desire to see Cambridge. He said it would be arranged. She said she would probably be in London soon. He said he hoped to see her there. Aunt Sarah stuck a pin in the baby's arm, whereupon Molly and Rat took Daphne aside and advised her to clear out of the house as soon as possible. 'It's unhealthy.'

'Oh,' said Daphne, 'but it's typically English.'

'Good gracious me!' said Rat.

At last she had her week in London with the relations of her friends in the Colony. Daphne had been told they were wealthy, and was surprised when the taxi drove her to a narrow house in a mean little side street which was otherwise lined with garages.

'Are you sure this is the right place?' she asked the driver.

'Twenty-five Champion Mews,' he said.

'That's right,' said Daphne. 'This must be it.'

Before Daphne had left the country Linda had re-marked, 'A house in Champion Mews. They must be rather rich. How I would adore a mews house.' Daphne remembered this.

The interior of the house was very winning. She re-adjusted her ideas, and at dinner was able to say to her hostess, 'What an adorable mews house.'

'Isn't it? We were so lucky — literally *everyone* was after it.'

Mrs. Pridham was middle-aged, and smart. Mr. Pridham was a plastic surgeon.

'I shan't make the mistake,' he said to Daphne, 'of asking you about all the dangers you encountered in darkest Africa.'

Daphne laughed.

'You must have a Season of course,' said Mrs. Prid-ham. 'Have you arranged anything?'

'I'm here for two years at least.' Then she remembered about the London Season, and said, 'No, I have nothing arranged. But my uncle has written to various friends.'

'It's getting a little late in the year,' said Mrs. Pridham.

'Really,' said Daphne, 'I just want to see England. I'd like to see London. I'd like to see the Tower, and Uncle Chakata's friends.'

'I shall take you to the Tower tomorrow afternoon,' said Mr. Pridham.

He did, and afterwards they went for a spin round Richmond and Kingston. He pulled up at a pleasant spot. 'Daphne,' he said, 'I love you.' And he pressed his lips of sixty summers to hers.

As soon as she could disengage herself, she casually wiped her mouth with her handkerchief — casually, for she did not want to hurt his feelings. However, she told him she was engaged to be married to someone in the Colony.

'Oh dear, I've done the wrong thing. Have I done the wrong thing?'

'Daphne is engaged to a lucky fellow in Africa,' he said at dinner that night. Mole was present. He looked at Daphne. She looked back helplessly. Mrs. Pridham looked at her husband, and said to Daphne, 'Before you do anything, you must have your London Season. Stay six weeks with us, do. I've brought out girls before. It's too late of course to do anything much but——'

'Do stay with us,' said Mr. Pridham.

Later, when Daphne explained the tale of her 'engagement' to Mole, he said, 'You can't stay with the Pridhams. I know someone else you can stay with, the mother of a friend of mine.'

Mrs. Pridham looked sad when Daphne told her she could not prolong her visit. For the rest of the week she unmistakably cast Daphne into her husband's way, frequently left them alone together, and often arranged to be picked up somewhere in the car, so that Daphne was obliged to dine with Mr. Pridham alone.

Daphne mentioned to Mole, 'She hasn't the least suspicion of what he's like. In fact, she seems to throw the man at me.'

'She wants to hot him up,' said Mole. 'There are plenty of women who behave like that. They get young girls to the house simply in order to give the old man ideas. Then they get rid of the girls.'

'Oh, I see.'

She went to stay as a paying guest with the mother of Mole's friend, Michael. It was arranged by letter.

Michael Casse was thin and gangling with an up-turned nose. He had been put to stockbroking with an uncle, but without success. He giggled a great deal. His mother, with whom he lived, took a perverse pride in his stupidity. 'Michael's hopelessness,' she told Daphne, 'is really . . .' During the war, his mother told her, she had been living in Berkshire. Michael came home on leave. She sent him out with the ration book one day after lunch to buy a packet of tea. He did not return until next morning. He handed his mother the tea, explaining that he had been held up by the connections.

'What connections?' said his mother.

'Oh, the trains, London, you know.'

And it transpired that he had gone áll the way to Fortnum's for the tea, it never having occurred to him that tea could be bought in the village, nor indeed anywhere else but Fortnum's. Daphne thought that *very* English.

Michael now lived with his mother in her flat in Regent's Park. Greta Casse was as gangling as her son, but she gangled effectively and always put her slender five foot ten into agreeable poses, so that even her stooping shoulders and hollow chest, her bony elbows akimbo, were becoming. She spoke with a nasal drawl. She lived on alimony and the rewards of keeping P.G.'s.

She took vastly too much money from Daphne, who suspected as much, but merely surmised that Greta Casse was, like her son, stupid, living in an unreal world where money hardly existed, and so one might easily charge one's P.G.'s too much. Daphne frequently slipped out to Lyons for a sandwich, so hungry did she go. She assumed at first that society women were simply not brought up to the food idea, but when she saw Greta Casse tucking in at anyone else's expense, she amended her opinion, and put Greta's domestic parsimony down to her vagueness about materialistic things. This was a notion which Greta fostered in various ways, such as always forgetting to give Daphne the change of a pound, or going off for the day and leaving nothing in the house for lunch.

That she was, however, a society woman, in a sense that Daphne's relations were not, was without doubt. Molly and Linda had been presented, it was true. And Daphne had seen photographs of her mother and Aunt Sarah beplumed and robed, in the days when these things were done properly. But they were decidedly not society women. Daphne mused often on Greta Casse, niece of a bishop and cousin of an earl, her distinctive qualities. She went to see Pooh-bah one week-end, and mentioned Greta Casse to a Miss Barrow, a notable spinster of the district who had come to tea. Daphne was surprised to learn that this woman, in her old mannish Burberry, her hands cracked with gardening, her face cracked with the weather, had been a contemporary of Greta's. They had been to various schools together, had been presented the same year.

'How odd,' Daphne remarked to Pooh-bah later, 'that two such different people as Mrs. Casse and Miss Barrow should have been brought up in the same way.'

He gave a verbal assent, 'I suppose so, yes,' but clearly he did not understand what she meant about it being odd.

Back she went to Regent's Park. Greta Casse arranged a dinner-party for Daphne at a West End restaurant, followed by an all-night session in a night club. About twenty young people were invited, most of them in their early teens, which made Daphne feel old, and she was not compensated by the presence of a few elders of Greta's generation. Michael came, of course. Englishman though he was, Daphne could not take him very seriously.

The party was followed by another, and that by another. 'Can't we invite Mole?' Daphne said.

'Well,' said Greta, 'the whole idea is for you to meet *new* people. But of course, if you like . . .'

The bill for these parties used up half of Daphne's annual allowance. Luncheons, at which she met numerous women friends of Greta's, used up the other half. Daphne longed to explain to Mrs. Casse that she had not understood what was involved by becoming her lodger. She did not want to be entertained, for she had merely counted on somewhere jolly to stay. Daphne had not the courage to put this to Greta who was so uncertain, precarious, slippery, indefinite and cold. She wrote to Chakata for money. 'Of course,' she wrote, 'when I've had my fun I'll take a job.'

'I hope you are seeing something of England,' he replied when he sent his cheque. 'My advice to you is to go on a coach tour. I hear they are excellent, and a great advance on my time, when there was nothing of that sort.' She rarely took much notice of Chakata's advice, for so much of it was inapplicable. 'Do introduce yourself to Merrivale at the bank,' he had written. 'He will give you sherry in the parlour, as he used to do me when I was your age.' On enquiring for Mr. Merrivale at the bank, Daphne was unsuccessful. 'Ever heard of a chap called Merrivale?' the clerks asked each other. 'Sure it's this branch?' they asked Daphne.

'Oh yes. He used to be the manager.'

'Sorry, madam, no-one's heard of him here. Must have been away back.'

'Oh, I see.'

Daphne got into the habit of ignoring Chakata's questions, 'Have you been to Hampton Court?' 'Did you call on Merrivale at the bank? He will give you sherry. . . .' 'Have you booked for a tour of England and Wales? I trust you are planning to see something of the English countryside?'

'I couldn't find that bootmaker in St. Paul's Churchyard,' she wrote to him, 'because it is all bombed.

Better stick to the usual place in Johannesburg. Anyway, I might not order the right boots.'

Soon, then, she made no reply to his specific requests and suggestions, but merely gave him an account of her parties, pepping them up for his benefit. He seemed not to read her letters properly, for he never referred to the parties.

Greta came back to the flat one afternoon with a toy poodle. 'He's yours,' she said to Daphne.

'How utterly perfect!' said Daphne, thinking it was a gift, and wanting to express her appreciation as near as possible in the vernacular.

'I *had* to have him for you,' said Greta, and went on to demand a hundred and ten guineas. Daphne ducked her face affectionately in the pet's curly coat to hide her dismay.

'We were so terribly lucky to get him,' Greta was saying. 'You see, he's not just a miniature — they're slightly bigger — he's a *toy*.'

Daphne gave her a cheque, and wrote to Chakata to say how expensive London was. She decided to take a job in the autumn, and to cut out the fortnight's motoring tour of the north with Molly, Rat and Mole which she had arranged to share with them.

Chakata sent her the money as an advance on her next quarterly allowance. 'Sorry can't do more. Fly has had a go at the horses, and you will have read about the tobacco crops.' She had not read about the blight, but a bad year was not an uncommon occurrence. She was surprised at Chakata's attitude, for she believed him to be fairly wealthy. Shortly after this she heard from friends in the Colony that Chakata's daughter and her husband who had gone to farm in Kenya, had been murdered by the Mau Mau. 'Chakata implored us not to tell you,' wrote her friend, 'but we thought you should know. Chakata is educating the two boys.'

It was the middle of May. Daphne had engaged to be Mrs. Casse's lodger till the end of June. However, she telephoned to Linda that she was returning to the country. Greta was out. Daphne packed and sat down courageously with Popcorn (the poodle) on her lap to await her return, and explain her financial predicament.

Michael came in first. He was carrying an empty bird-cage and a cardboard box with holes in it. On opening the box a bird flew out in a panic.

'A budgerigar,' said Michael. 'I expect they fly about wild where you've come from. They talk, you know. It's frightened at the moment, but when they get used to you, they talk.' He giggled.

The bird was perched on a lampshade. Daphne caught it and put it in the cage. It had a lavender breast.

'It's for you,' Michael said. 'Mummy sent me home with it. She bought it for you. It says "Come here, darling" and "Go to hell", and things like that.'

'I really don't want it,' said Daphne in despair.

'Peep, peep, peep,' said Michael to the bird, 'say hallo, say hallo. Say come here darling.'

It sat on the floor of the cage and moved only its head from side to side.

'Really,' said Daphne, 'I have no money. I'm hard up. I can't afford your mother's birds. I'm just waiting to say goodbye to her.'

'No,' said Michael.

'Yes,' said Daphne.

'Listen,' he said. 'Take my advice and clear out now before she comes back. If you tell her this to her face there's bound to be hell.' He giggled weakly, poured himself a drink of brandy which his mother had watered, and said, 'Shall I get you a taxi now? She'll be back in half an hour.'

'No, I'll wait,' said Daphne, and ran her hand nervously through the poodle's curls.

'There was nearly a court action one time,' said Michael, 'about another girl. Mummy was supposed to have given two balls for her, but she didn't or something, and the girl's people got worked up. I think Mummy spent the money on something else, or something.' He giggled.

'Oh, I see.' Daphne went and telephoned to Mole and asked him to call for her when he left his office.

Greta arrived, and when she had taken in the situation she sent Michael from the room.

'I must tell you,' said Greta to Daphne, 'that what you are proposing is illegal. You realise that, don't you?'

'I can give you a week's money in lieu of notice,' Daphne said, 'and a little extra.'

'You agreed to stay till the end of June, my dear. I have it in black and white.' This was true. Daphne realised how deliberately her letter of confirmation from the country had been extracted from her.

'My uncle has had some unforeseen expenses. My cousins were murdered by the Mau Mau, and their sons——'

'I'm sorry, my dear, but one just can't be sentimental. It's not like taking in ordinary lodgers. A Season is a Season, and one can't get another girl at this time of the year. Look what I've done for you. Parties, the races, meeting important people. . . . No, sorry, I can't consider releasing you from the obligation. I've arranged a cocktail party at Claridge's for you next week. After all, I don't make anything out of it. Mercy Slater charges fifteen hundred to bring a girl out.'

This put Daphne off her stroke, it prompted her to haggle: 'Lady Slater gives balls for her debs.'

Greta rapidly got in: 'You surely didn't expect the full deb process in your position?'

'Mole is calling for me,' Daphne said.

'I don't want to keep you against your will, Daphne. But if you leave now you must compensate me fully. Then, if you want to go away, go away.'

'Go'way. Go'way, go to hell,' said the budgerigar, which had now risen to its perch.

'And then there's the bird,' said she. 'I bought it for you this afternoon. I thought you'd be thrilled.' She began to weep.

'I don't want it,' said Daphne.

'All my girls have adored their pets,' Greta said.

'Come here darling,' said the bird. 'Go'way, go to hell.'

Greta was doing a sum. 'The bird is twenty guineas. Then there's the extra clothes I've ordered——'

'Go'way. Go'way,' said the bird.

Mole arrived. Daphne placed a cheque for twenty pounds on the hall table and slipped down to his car, leaving him to cope with her bags. 'You will hear from my solicitors,' Greta called after her.

Michael was hanging about in the hall. He took the

scene calmly. He giggled at Daphne, then went to help Mole with the luggage.

They had been driving for ten minutes before they had to stop for a traffic light. Then, when the engine stopped, Daphne heard the budgerigar chirping at the back of the car.

'You've brought the bird!' she said.

'Yes. Isn't it yours? Michael told me it was yours.'

'I'll ring the pet shop,' she said, 'and ask them to take it back. Do you think Greta Casse will sue me?'

'She hasn't a hope,' said Mole. 'Forget it.'

Daphne rang the pet shop next morning from the country.

'This is Mrs. Casse speaking,' she said with a nasal voice. 'I bought a budgerigar from you yesterday. So silly of me, I've forgotten what I paid you, and I'd like to know, just for my records.'

'Mrs. Greta Casse?'

'That's right.'

'I don't think we sold a budgie yesterday, Mrs. Casse. Just a moment, I'll enquire.'

After a pause another, more authoritative, person came on the line. 'You're enquiring about a budgerigar, Mrs. Casse?'

'Yes, I bought it yesterday,' said Daphne through her nose.

'Not from us, Mrs. Casse — oh, and by the way, Mrs. Casse . . .'

'Yes,' twanged Daphne.

'While you're on the phone, I'd like to mention the account.'

'Of course. How much is it? I'll send a cheque.'

'Eighty guineas — that's of course including the toy poodle.'

'Ah, yes. What exactly was the sum for the poodle? I'm so scatty about these things.'

'The poodle was sixty. Then there was an amount last October——'

'Thanks. I'm sure it's quite correct. I'll send a cheque.'

'You have stolen that bird, *I* know,' said Aunt Sarah that afternoon, giving the cage a shove.

'No,' said Daphne, 'I paid for it.'

In the spring of nineteen forty-seven Linda died of a disease of the blood. At the funeral a short man of about forty-five introduced himself to Daphne. He was Martin Grindy, the barrister who had been Linda's lover.

He gave Daphne his card. 'Would you come some time and talk about Linda?'

'Yes, of course.'

'Next week?'

'Well, I'm teaching. But when school breaks up I'll write to you.'

She wrote during the Easter holidays, and met him for lunch a few days later.

He said, 'I miss Linda.'

'Yes, I'm sure you must.'

'The trouble is, you see, I'm a married man.'

She thought him attractive and understood why Linda had always felt urgently about keeping her appointments with him.

In the summer she started to replace Linda as Martin's lover. They met in London at week-ends and more frequently in the summer holidays.

Daphne was teaching at a private school in Henley. She lived with Pooh-bah and a middle-aged house-keeper whom they had persuaded into service, the old servant, Clara, having died, and Aunt Sarah having been removed to a nursing home.

Mole had married, and Daphne missed his frequent visits, and the long drives in his car. Until she met Martin Grindy her life was enlivened only by the visiting art-master at the school, who came down twice a week.

Martin's wife, several years older than he, lived in Surrey and was always ill with a nervous complaint.

'There's no question of a divorce,' Martin said. 'My wife's against it on religious grounds, and though I myself don't share these principles I feel a personal obligation towards her.'

'Oh, I see.'

They spent their time in his flat in Kensington. There was a heatwave. They bathed in the Serpentine.

Sometimes, if his wife was specially ill, he would be summoned to the country. Daphne stayed alone in the flat or wandered round the shops.

'This year,' said Martin, 'she has been more ill than usual. But next year if she's better, I hope to take you to Austria.'

'Next year,' she said, 'I am supposed to be returning to Africa.'

Earlier Chakata had written, 'Old Tuys has had a stroke. He is up now, but very feeble in his mind.' Since then, he had seemed less keen on Daphne's return. Daphne thought this odd, for previously he had been wont to write when sending her news of the farm, 'You will see many changes when you return,' or, when mentioning affairs at the dorp, 'There's a new doctor. You'll like him.' But in his last letter he had said, 'There have been changes in the educational system. You will find many changes if you return.' Sometimes she thought Chakata was merely becoming forgetful. 'I'm trying to make the most of my stay in England,' she wrote, 'but travelling is very expensive. I doubt if I shall see anything of Europe before my return.' Chakata, in his next letter, did not touch on the question. He said, 'Old Tuys just sits about on the stoep. Poor old chap, he is incapable of harm now. He is rather pathetic on the whole.'

At the end of the summer Daphne's lover took his wife to Torquay. Daphne wandered about Kensington alone for a few days, then went back to Pooh-bah. She took him for walks. She asked him to lend her some money so that she might spend a week in Paris. He replied that he didn't really see the necessity. Next day the housekeeper told her of a man in the village who would give her thirty pounds for the poodle. Daphne had grown fond of the dog. She refused the offer, then wrote to her lover in Torquay to ask him to lend her the money to go to Paris. She received a post-card from Martin, with no mention of her request. 'Will be back in London 1st week October,' he wrote on the card.

Term started at the beginning of October. That week Martin's wife turned up and demanded of Pooh-bah Daphne's whereabouts. She was directed to the school, and on confronting Daphne there, made a scene.

Later, the headmistress was highly offensive to Daphne, who straightway resigned. The headmistress relented, for she was short of staff. 'I am only thinking of the girls,' she explained. Hugh, the visiting art-master, suggested to Daphne that she might find a better job in London. She left that night. Pooh-bah was furious. 'Who's going to attend to things on Mrs. Vesey's day off?' Daphne realised why he had not wished her to go to Paris.

'You could marry her,' Daphne suggested. 'Then she'd be on duty all the time.'

He did this in fact, within a month. Daphne settled in a room in Bayswater, poorly furnished for the price; but on the other hand the landlady was willing to take the poodle.

Martin Grindy traced her to that place.

'I don't like your wife,' she said.

'I'm afraid she got hold of your letter. What can I give you? What can I do for you? What can I possibly say?'

Besides teaching art to schoolchildren, Hugh Fuller painted. He took Daphne to his studio in Earl's Court, where she sat and reflectively pulled the stuffing even further out of the torn upholstery of the armchair.

Quite decidedly, she said, she would not come and live with him, but she hoped they would always be friends.

He thought he had made a mistake in putting the proposition to her before making love, so he made moves to repair his error.

Daphne screamed. He looked surprised.

'You see,' she explained, 'I've got nerves, frightfully, at the moment.'

He took her frequently to Soho, and sometimes to

parties where, for the first time, she entered a world in the existence of which she had previously disbelieved. Here the poets *did* have long hair, and painters wore beards, and, what was more, two of the men wore bracelets and earrings. One group of four girls lived all together in two rooms with a huge old negress. Among Hugh's acquaintance were those who looked upon him with scorn for his art-teaching, those who considered this activity harmless in view of his lack of talent, and those who admired him for his industry as much as his generosity.

Daphne found this company very relaxing to her nerves.

No-one asked her the usual questions about Africa, and what was more surprising, no-one made advances to her, not even Hugh. Daphne was teaching at a Council school. On half-holidays in spring she would sometimes meet Hugh and his friends, and regardless of the staring streets, would straggle with them along the pavements, leap on and off buses, to the current art show. There, it was clear to Daphne that Hugh's friends occupied a world which she could never penetrate. But she came to be more knowing about pictures. It may have been the art-master in Hugh, as one of his friends suggested, but he loved to inform Daphne as to form, line, light, masses, pigments.

Her cousin Mole looked her up one day. He told her that Michael, the silly son of that Greta Casse at Regent's Park, had married a woman ten years his senior, and was emigrating to the Colony. Daphne was affected with an attack of longing for the Colony, more dire than any of those bouts of homesickness which she had yet experienced.

'I shall have to go back there soon,' she said to Mole. 'I've saved enough for the fare. It's a good thought to know I can go any time I please.'

One night Daphne and Hugh were drinking in a pub in Soho with his friends, when suddenly there fell a hush. Daphne looked round to see why everyone's eyes were on a slight very dark man in his early forties, who had just entered the bar. After a moment, everyone started talking again, some giggled, and continued to glance at the man who had come in.

'That's Ralph Mercer,' one of Hugh's friends whispered to Daphne.

'Who?'

'Ralph Mercer, the novelist. He was at school with Hugh, I believe. Rather a *popular* writer.'

'Oh, I see,' said Daphne, 'he looks as if he might be popular.'

Hugh was collecting drinks at the bar. The novelist saw him, and they spoke together for a while. Presently Hugh brought him to be introduced. The novelist sat next to Daphne. 'You remind me of someone I used to know from Africa,' he said.

'I come from Africa,' said Daphne.

Hugh asked him, 'Often come here?'

'No, it was just, you know, I was passing . . .'

One of the girls chuckled, a deep masculine sound. 'A whim,' she said.

When he had gone Hugh said, 'He's rather sweet, isn't he, considering how famous . . .'

'Did you hear him,' said an oldish man, 'when he said, "Speaking as an artist . . ." Rather funny, that, I thought.'

'Well, he *is* an artist in the sense,' said Hugh,

'that——' But his words were obliterated by the others' derision.

A few days later Hugh said to Daphne, 'I've heard from Ralph Mercer.'

'Who?'

'That novelist we met in the pub. He writes to know if I'll give him your address.'

'Why's that, do you think?'

'He likes you, I suppose.'

'Is he married?'

'No. He lives with his mother. Actually I've sent him your address. Do you mind?'

'Yes, I do. I'm not a name and address to be passed round. I'm afraid I don't wish to see you again.'

'You know,' said Hugh, 'I'm glad it never came to an affair between us. You see, Daphne, I'm not entirely a woman's man.'

'I don't know what to say,' she said.

'I hope you will like Ralph Mercer. He's very well-off. Very interesting, too.'

'I shall refuse to see him,' said Daphne.

Her association with Ralph Mercer lasted two years. Her infatuation was as gluttonous as her status as his mistress was high among the few writers and numerous film people who kept him company. She had a grey-carpeted flat in Hampstead, with the best and latest Swedish furniture. Ralph's male friends wooed her, telephoned all day, came with flowers and theatre tickets.

For the first three months Ralph was with her constantly. She told him of her childhood, of Chakata, the farm, the dorp, Donald Cloete, the affair of Old

Tuys. He demanded more and more. 'I need to know your entire background, every detail. Love is an expedition of discovery into unexplored territory.' To Daphne this approach had such force of originality that it sharpened her memory. She remembered incidents which had been latent for fifteen years or more. She sensed the sort of thing that delighted him; the feud, for instance, between Old Tuys and Chakata; revenge and honour. One day after receiving a letter from Chakata she was able to tell him the last sentence of Donald Cloete's story: he had died of drink. She offered him this humble contribution with pride, for it showed that she, too, though no novelist, possessed a sense of character and destiny. 'Always,' she said, 'I would ask him was he drunk or sober, and he always told the truth.' Later in the day, when the thought of Donald's death came suddenly to her mind, she cried for a space.

News came that Mrs. Chakata had followed Donald to the grave, and for the same cause. Daphne laid this information on the altar. The novelist was less impressed than on the former occasion. 'Old Tuys has been done out of his revenge,' Daphne added for good measure, although she was aware that Old Tuys had been silly and senile since his stroke. One of her friends in the Colony had written to say that Mrs. Chakata had long since ceased to have the pistol by her side: 'Old Tuys takes no notice of her. He's forgotten what it was all about.'

'Death has cheated Old Tuys,' said Daphne.

'Very melodramatic,' he commented.

Ralph began to disappear for days and weeks without warning. In a panic, Daphne would telephone to his mother. 'I don't know where he is,' Mrs. Mercer would say. 'Really, dear, he's like that. It's very trying.'

Much later, his mother was to tell Daphne, 'I love my son, but quite honestly I don't *like* him.' Mrs. Mercer was an intensely religious woman. Ralph loved his mother but did not like her. He was frequently seized by nervy compulsions and superstitions.

'I must,' said Ralph, 'write. I need solitude to write. That is why I go away.'

'Oh, I see,' said Daphne.

'If you say that again I'll hit you.' And though she did not repeat the words, he did, just then, hit her.

Afterwards she said, 'If only you would say goodbye before you leave I wouldn't mind so much. It's the suddenness that upsets me.'

'All right then. I'm going away tonight.'

'Where are you going? Where?'

'Why,' he said, 'don't you go back to Africa?'

'I don't want to.' Her obsession with Ralph had made Africa seem a remote completed thing.

His next book was more successful than any he had written. The film was in preparation. He told Daphne he adored her really, and he quite saw that he led her a hell of a life. That was what it meant to be tied up with an artist, he was afraid.

'It's worth it,' Daphne said, 'and I think I can help you in some ways.'

He thought so too just at that moment, for it occurred to him that his latest book was all of it written during his association with Daphne. 'I think we should get married,' he said.

Next day he left the flat and went abroad. Now,

after two years her passion for him was not diminished, neither were her misery and dread.

Three weeks later he wrote from his mother's address to suggest that she moved out of the flat. He would make a settlement.

She telephoned to his mother's house. 'He won't speak to you,' his mother said. 'I'm ashamed of him, to tell the truth.'

Daphne took a taxi to the house.

'He's upstairs writing,' his mother said. 'He's going away somewhere else tomorrow. I hope he stays away, to tell the truth.'

'I must see him,' said Daphne.

His mother said, 'He makes me literally ill. I'm too old for this sort of thing, my dear. God bless you.'

She went and called upstairs, 'Ralph, come down a moment, please.' She waited till she heard his footsteps on the stairs, then she disappeared quickly.

'Go away,' said Ralph to Daphne. 'Go away and leave me in peace.'

III

Daphne arrived in the Colony during the rainy season. The rains made Chakata's rheumatism bad. He talked a lot about his rheumatism, would question her about England without listening to her replies.

'The West End is badly bombed,' she said.

'It gets me in the groin when I turn in bed,' he answered.

Various neighbours looked in to see Daphne. The young had married, and some who called were new to her.

'There's a chap out from England farming over at the south, says he knows you,' said Chakata. 'Name Cash, I think.'

'Casse,' said Daphne, 'Michael Casse. Is that the name?'

'This stuff the doctor gives me's no good. In fact it makes me worse.'

Another tobacco manager was living in the house Old Tuys had occupied. Old Tuys was at the farmhouse with Chakata. He sat in his corner of the stoep, talking nonsense to himself, or ambled about the farm. Chakata was annoyed when Old Tuys walked about, for he himself could barely hobble. 'A pathetic case,' he would say as Old Tuys strolled by, 'he's got his limbs, but he hasn't got his faculties. I at least have my faculties.' He preferred to see Old Tuys in his chair on the stoep. Then Chakata would say, 'You know, after all these years, I have a soft spot for Old Tuys.'

Old Tuys ate noisily. Chakata did not seem to mind. It struck Daphne that she was useless to Chakata now that she was no longer a goad for Old Tuys. She decided to stay at the farm no longer than a month. She would get a job in the Capital.

The third day after her arrival there was a break in the rains. She wandered round the sunny farm all morning, and after lunch set off northward for Makata's kraal. The new tobacco manager agreed very happily to come with his car and fetch her later on.

She had become unused to trekking any distance. Her energy ebbed after the first mile. A cloud of locusts caught her attention and automatically she stopped to watch anxiously whether the swarm would settle on Chakata's mealies or miss them. It passed over. She sat to rest on a stone, disturbing a baby lizard. 'Go'way. Go'way,' she heard.

Daphne called aloud, 'God help me. Life is unbearable.'

A house-boy came running to Chakata who was round by the tobacco shed resting on two sticks.

'Baas Tuys is gone to shoot buck. The piccanin say he take a gun to shoot buck.'

'Who? What?'

'Baas Tuys with gun.'

'Where? Which way?'

'Is gone by north. The piccanin have seen him. Was after lunch piccanin say, he talk that he go to shoot buck.'

A few more natives had gathered round.

'Run, quick, all of you. Get that gun off Old Tuys. Fetch him back.'

They looked at him hesitantly. It was not every day that a native was instructed to wrest a gun from the hands of a white man.

'Go, you fools. Run.'

They returned slowly and fearfully half an hour later. Chakata had hobbled to the end of the paddock to meet them.

'Where's Tuys? Did you get him?'

They did not answer at first. Then one of them pointed to the path through the maize where Old Tuys was staggering home, exhausted, dragging something behind him.

'Go and pick her up,' ordered Chakata.

'I got me a buck,' said Old Tuys, looking with pride

at the company. 'Man, there's life in the old dog yet. I got us a buck.'

He looked closely at Chakata. He could not understand why Chakata was not impressed.

'We have buck for dinner, man Chakata,' he said.

Burials follow quickly after death in the Colony, for the temperature does not allow of delay. The inquest was held and Daphne was buried next day. Michael Casse came over for the funeral to the cemetery outside the dorp.

'I knew her quite well, you know. She stayed with my mother,' he said to Chakata. 'My mother gave her a bird, or something like that.' He giggled. Chakata looked at him curiously and saw that the man was not smiling.

Chakata was being helped into the car. 'I must see a specialist,' he said.

Ralph Mercer was moved when he heard the news. It was like the confirmation of something one knew already. Daphne had begun to live when he had first met her, and when she had gone she had been in a sense dead. He tried to explain this to his mother.

'Like flowers, you know, in the garden. One can't say they really *exist* unless one's looking at them. Or take——'

'Flowers, garden . . . You are talking of a human soul.'

It was a year later that Ralph felt a crisis in his work. His books were selling, but on the other hand they were not taken seriously enough by serious people. All his novels had ended happily. He decided to write a tragedy.

He ranged his experience for a tragedy. He thought of, and rejected as too banal, the domestic ruptures of his friends past and present. He rejected the story of his mother, widowed young, disappointed in her son, but still pushing on: that was too personal. He thought of Daphne. That might lead to something both exotic and tragic. He recalled her stories of Old Tuys and Chakata, the theme of the lifelong feud. He took a ticket on a plane to the Colony in order to obtain background material at first hand.

Almost immediately he arrived in the Colony he found himself beset by admirers. He had never before been so celebrated and popular in his person. He was invited to Government House. Dinners were given in his honour, and people drove in through swollen rivers from outlying districts to attend them. He had to pick and choose amongst the invitations he received. Everyone with a white skin had heard of, if they had not read, Ralph Mercer. Moreover, seated among this company on wide verandahs after dinner he could look round without catching the cool eye of some critic, some frightful man whom the public hardly ever heard of, but who, at home, was always present at parties of this sort, and who put Ralph out. He began to think he had vastly underrated the intelligence of his public.

'I have been thinking of changing my style. I've been thinking of writing a tragedy.'

'Good Lord,' said the retired Brigadier whom he had addressed, 'you don't want to do that.'

Everyone said the same.

Another thing everyone said was, 'Why don't you

settle here?' or 'Why don't you take a place and live here for part of the year? It's the only way to avoid the heavy taxes.'

At the Club he had met Michael Casse who had come up to the Capital to see the Land Bank about a loan.

'My wife adores your books,' said Michael. He giggled. Ralph wondered for a moment if Michael was a critic.

'We have a mutual friend,' said Michael, 'or rather *had*. Daphne du Toit. I went to her funeral.' He giggled.

'The reason I've come out here is to see her grave,' said Ralph defensively. 'And to talk to her uncle.'

'Got a car?' said Michael. 'If not I'll drive you down. I live near them.' Ralph realised that Michael's giggle was a nervous tic.

'I might settle in the Colony — seven months in the year, you know,' he confided.

'There's a nice place near us,' said Michael. 'It's coming up for sale soon.'

Ralph had been two months in the Colony, had toured the country, had been shown all the interesting spots, and met the enjoyable people, when at last he accepted Michael's invitation to stay at his farm.

'Are you writing anything at the moment?' said Michael's wife.

'No, but I'm collecting material.'

'Oh, will it be about the Colony?'

'It's difficult to say.'

He was not sure now that the Daphne idea would be as appealing as he had thought. He could not envisage his public, especially that section which he had recently met at close quarters, appreciating such a theme.

Michael showed him over the farm which was up for sale. Ralph said he would almost certainly take it.

They went to see Chakata and Ralph spoke of Daphne. Chakata said, 'Why didn't she settle down in England? Why did she come back?'

'I suppose she wanted to,' said Michael, and giggled.

Chakata spoke of his rheumatism. He hobbled out on the stoep and called for drinks. As they followed, Ralph noticed a lanky old man seated in the corner, muttering to himself.

He enquired of Chakata. 'Is that Mr. Tuys? Daphne told me about Mr. Tuys.'

Chakata said, 'Bad year for maize. I shan't live long.'

Michael drove Ralph down to the cemetery. His wife had suggested: 'Leave him alone for a while in the cemetery. I think he was in love with the girl.' Michael respected his wife's delicacy. He giggled, left Ralph at the graveside, and explaining that he had some errands to do in the village, said he would be back by and by.

'You won't be long,' said Ralph, 'will you?'

'Oh no,' said Michael.

'There seem to be a lot of mosquitoes about here. Is it a fever area?'

'Oh no.' He giggled and went.

After Ralph had looked at the inscription, 'Daphne du Toit, 1922 – 1950', he walked up and down. He looked blankly at the gravestones and noticed one inscribed 'Donald Cloete'. This name seemed familiar, but he could not remember in what way. Perhaps it was someone Daphne had talked about.

'Go'way, go'way.'

That was the bird, just behind Daphne's grave. She had often mentioned the bird.

'It says go'way, go'way.'

'Well, what about it?' he had said to her irritably, for sometimes she had appeared to him, as in a revelation, a personified Stupidity.

She would tell him, 'There's a bird that says "Go'way, go'way"', without connecting the information with any particular event; she would expect him to be interested, as if he were an ornithologist, not an author.

'Go'way, go'way,' said the bird behind Daphne's grave.

He heard the bird at some time during each day for the next six weeks while he was completing his tour of the rural spaces. He was glad to return to the Capital, and to be free of its voice. Relaxing in the Club, it was as though the bird had never existed.

However, he went with the Governor for a round of golf:

'Go'way. Go'way. . . .'

He booked a seat on the plane to England for the following week. He met Michael once more by chance at Williams Hotel.

'That farm,' said Michael '— someone else has made an offer. You'd better settle right away.'

'I don't want it,' said Ralph. 'I don't want to stay here.'

They sat on the stoep drinking highballs. Beyond the mosquito netting was the bird.

'Can you hear that go-away bird?' said Ralph.

Michael listened obediently.

'No, I can't say I can.' He giggled, and Ralph wanted to hit him.

'I hear it everywhere,' said Ralph. 'I don't like it. That's why I'm going.'

'Good Lord. Keen on bird-life, are you?'

'No, not particularly.'

'Ralph Mercer isn't going to buy the farm,' Michael told his wife that evening.

'I thought it was settled.'

'No, he's going home. He isn't coming back. He says he doesn't like the birds here.'

'I wish you could cure that giggle, Michael. What did you say he doesn't like?'

'The birds.'

'*Birds*. Is he an ornithologist then?'

'No, I think he's R.C.'

'A *man*, darling, who studies birds.'

'Oh! Well, no, he said no, he's not particularly interested in birds.'

'How extraordinary,' she said.

Daisy Overend

IT is hardly ever that I think of her, but sometimes, if I happen to pass Clarges Street or Albemarle Street on a sunny afternoon, she comes to mind. Or if, in a little crowd waiting to cross the road I hear behind me two women meet, and the one exclaim:

'Darling!' (or 'Bobbie!' or 'Goo!') and the other answer: 'Goo!' (or 'Billie!' or 'Bobbie!' or 'Darling!') — if I hear these words, spoken in a certain trill which betokens the period 1920–9, I know that I have by chance entered the world of Daisy Overend, Bruton Street, W.1.

Ideally, these Bobbies and Darlings are sheathed in short frocks, the hems of which dangle about their knees like seaweed, the waistlines of which encircle their hips, loose and effortless, following the droop of shoulder and mouth. Ideally, the whole is upheld by a pair of shiny silk stockings of a bright hue known as, but not resembling a, peach.

But in reality it is only by the voice you can tell them. The voice harks back to days bright and young and unredeemable whence the involuntary echoes arise — *Billie!* . . . *Goo!* . . . *heavenly!* . . . *divine!* like the motto and crest which adorn the letter paper of a family whose silver is pawned and forgotten.

Daisy Overend, small, imperious, smart, was to my

mind the flower and consummation of her kind, and this is not to discount the male of the species *Daisy Overend*, with his wee face, blue eyes, bad teeth and nerves. But if you have met Mrs. Overend, you have as good as met him too, he is so unlike her, and yet so much her kind.

I met her, myself, in the prodigious and lovely summer of 1947. Very charming she was. A tubular skirt clung to her hips, a tiny cap to her hair, and her hair clung, bronzed and shingled, to her head, like the cup of a toy egg of which her face was the other half. Her face was a mere lobe. Her eyes were considered to be expressive and they expressed avarice in various forms; the pupils were round and watchful. Mrs. Overend engaged me for three weeks to help her with some committee work. As you will see, we parted in three days.

I found that literature and politics took up most of Daisy's days and many of her nights. She wrote a regular column in a small political paper and she belonged to all the literary societies. Thus, it was the literature of politics and the politics of literature which occupied Daisy, and thus she bamboozled many politicians who thought she was a writer, and writers who believed her to be a political theorist. But these activities failed to satisfy, that is to say, intoxicate her.

Now, she did not drink. I saw her sipping barley water while her guests drank her gin. But Daisy had danced the Charleston in her youth with a royal prince, and of this she assured me several times, speaking with swift greed while an alcoholic look came over her.

'Those times were divine,' she boozily concluded, 'they were ripping.' And I realised she was quite drunk

with the idea. Normally as precise as a bird, she reached
out blunderingly for the cigarettes, knocking the whole
lot over. Literature and politics failed to affect her in
this way, though she sat on many committees. Therefore she had taken — it is her expression — two lovers:
one an expert, as she put it, on politics, and the other a
poet.

The political expert, Lotti, was a fair Central European, an exiled man. The skin of his upper lip was
drawn taut across his top jaw; this gave Lotti the
appearance, together with his high cheekbones, of having had his face lifted. But it was not so; it was a natural
defect which made his smile look like a baring of the
teeth. He was perhaps the best of the lot that I met at
Daisy Overend's.

Lotti could name each member of every Western
Cabinet which had sat since the Treaty of Versailles.
Daisy found this invaluable for her monthly column.
Never did Lotti speak of these men but with contempt.
He was a member of three shadow cabinets.

On the Sunday which, as it turned out, was my last
day with Daisy, she laid aside her library book and said
to Lotti:

'I'm bored with Cronin.'

Lotti, to whom all statesmen were as the ash he was
just then flicking to the floor, looked at her all amazed.

'Daisy, mei gurl, you crazy?' he said.

'A Cronin!' he said, handing me an armful of air to
convey the full extent of his derision, 'She is bored with
a Cronin.'

At that moment, Daisy's vexed misunderstood expression reminded me that her other lover, the poet

Tom Pfeffer, had brought the same look to her face two days before. When, rushing into the flat as was her wont, she said, gasping, to Tom:

'Things have been happening in the House.'

Tom, who was reading the Notebooks of Malte Laurids Brigge, looked up.

'Nothing's been happening in the house,' he assured her.

Tom Pfeffer is dead now. Mrs. Overend told me the story of how she rescued him from lunacy, and I think Tom believed this. It is true she had prevented his being taken to a mental home for treatment.

The time came when Tom wanted, on an autumn morning, a ticket to Burton-on-Trent to visit a friend, and he wanted this more than he wanted a room in Mrs. Overend's flat and regular meals. In his own interests she refused, obliterating the last traces of insurrection by giving Lotti six pound notes, clean from the bank, in front of Tom.

How jealous Tom Pfeffer was of Lotti, how indifferent was Lotti to him! But on this last day that I spent with Mrs. Overend, the poet was fairly calm, although there were signs of the awful neurotic dance of his facial muscles which were later to distort him utterly before he died insane.

Daisy was preparing for a party, the reason for my presence on a Sunday, and for the arrival at five o'clock of her secretary Miss Rilke, a displaced European, got cheap. When anyone said to Daisy 'Is she related to the poet Rilke?' Daisy replied, 'Oh, I should *think* so,' indignant almost, that it should be doubted.

'Be an angel,' said Daisy to Miss Rilke when she

arrived, 'run down to the café and get me two packets of twenty. Is it still raining? How priceless the weather is. Take my awning.'

'Awning?'

'*Umbrella, umbrella, umbrella,*' said Daisy, jabbing her finger at it fractiously.

Like ping-pong, Miss Rilke's glance met Lotti's, and Lotti's hers. She took the umbrella and went.

'What are you looking at?' Daisy said quickly to Lotti.

'Nothing,' said Tom Pfeffer, thinking he was being addressed and looking up from his book.

'Not you,' said Daisy.

'Do you mean me?' I said.

'No,' she said, and kept her peace.

Miss Rilke returned to say that the shop would give Mrs. Overend no more credit.

'This is the end,' said Daisy as she shook out the money from her purse. 'Tell them I'm livid.'

'Yes,' said Miss Rilke, looking at Lotti.

'What are you looking at?' Daisy demanded of her.

'Looking at?'

'Have you got the right money?' Daisy said.

'Yes.'

'Well, go.'

'I think,' said Daisy when she had gone, 'she's a bit dotty owing to her awful experiences.'

Nobody replied.

'Don't you think so?' she said to Lotti.

'Could be,' said Lotti.

Tom looked up suddenly. 'She's bats,' he hastened to say, 'the silly bitch is bats.'

Daisy Overend

As soon as Miss Rilke returned Daisy started becking and calling in preparation for her party. Her papers which lay on every plane surface in the room were moved into her bedroom in several piles.

The drawing-room was furnished in a style which in many ways anticipated the members' room at the Institute of Contemporary Arts. Mrs. Overend had recently got rid of her black-and-orange striped divans, cushions and sofas. In their place were curiously cut slabs, polygons and three-legged manifestations of Daisy Overend's personality, done in El Greco's colours. As Daisy kept on saying, no two pieces were alike, and each was a contemporary version of a traditional design.

In her attempt to create a Contemporary interior she was, I felt, successful, and I was quite dazzled by its period charm. 'A rare old Contemporary piece,' some curio dealer, not yet born, might one day aver of Daisy's citrine settle or her blue glass-topped telephone table, adding in the same breath and pointing elsewhere, 'A genuine brass-bracket gas jet, nineteenth century'.... But I was dreaming, and Daisy was working, shifting things, blowing the powdery dust off things. She trotted and tripped amid the pretty jigsaw puzzle of her furniture, making a clean sweep of letters, bills, pamphlets and all that suggested a past or a future, with one exception. This was the photograph of Daisy Overend, haughty and beplumed in presentation dress, queening it over the Contemporary prospect of the light-grey grand piano.

Sometimes, while placing glasses and plates now here, now there, Daisy stopped short to take in the effect; and at this sign we all of us did the same. I realised then how silently and well did Daisy induce people to humour her. I discovered that the place was charged on a high voltage with the constant menace of a scene.

'I've put the papers on your bed,' said Miss Rilke from the bedroom.

'Is *she* saying something?' said Daisy, as if it were the last straw.

'Yes,' said Miss Rilke in a loud voice.

'They are not to go on my bed,' replied Daisy, having heard her in the first place.

'She's off her head, my dear,' said the poet to his mistress, 'putting your papers on your bed.'

'Go and see what she's doing,' said Daisy to me.

I went, and there found Miss Rilke moving the papers off the bed on to the floor. I was impressed by the pinkness of Daisy's bedroom. Where on earth did she get her taste in pink? Now this was not in the Contemporary style, nor was it in the manner of Daisy's heyday, the nineteen-twenties. The kidney-shaped dressing table was tricked out with tulle, unhappy spoiled stuff which cold cream had long ago stained, cigarettes burned, and various jagged objects ripped. In among the folds the original colour had survived here and there, and this fervid pink reminded me of a colour I had seen before, a pink much loved and worn by the women of the Malay colony at Capetown.

No, this was not a bedroom of the 'twenties; it belonged, surely, to the first ten years of the century: an Edwardian bedroom. But then, even then, it was hardly the sort of room Daisy would have inherited, since neither her mother nor her grandmother had kicked her height at the Gaiety. No, it was Daisy's own inarticulate exacting instinct which had bestowed on this room its frilly bed, its frilly curtains, the silken and sorry roses on its mantelpiece and its all-but-perished powder puffs. And all in pink, and all in pink. I did not solve the mystery of Daisy's taste in bedrooms, not then nor at any time. For, whenever I provide a category of time and place for her, the evidence is in default. A plant of the 'twenties, she is also the perpetrator of that vintage bedroom. A lingering limb of the old leisured class, she is also the author of that pink room.

I devoted the rest of the evening to the destruction of Daisy's party, I regret to say, and the subversion of her purpose in giving it.

Her purpose was the usual thing. She had joined a new international guild, and wanted to sit on the committee. Several Members of Parliament, a director of a mineral-water factory, a Brigadier-General who was also an Earl, a retired Admiral, some wives, a few women journalists, were expected. In addition, she had asked some of her older friends, those who were summoned to all her parties and whom she called her 'basics'; they were the walkers-on or the chorus of Daisy's social drama. There was also a Mr. Jamieson, who was not invited but who played an unseen part as the chairman of the committee. He did not want Mrs. Overend to sit on his committee. We were therefore assembled, though few guessed it, to inaugurate a campaign to remove from office this Mr. Jamieson, whose colleagues and acquaintances presently began to arrive.

Parted from the drawing-room by folding doors was

an ante-room leading out of the flat. I was put in charge of this room where a buffet had been laid. Here Daisy had repaired, when dressing for the party, to change her stockings. It was her habit to dress in every room in the house, anxiously moving from place to place. Miss Rilke had been sent on a tour of the premises to collect the discarded clothes, the comb, the lipstick from the various stations of Daisy's journey; but the secretary had overlooked, on a table in the centre of this ante-room, a pair of black satin garters a quarter of a century old, each bearing a very large grimy pink disintegrating rosette.

Just before the first guests began to arrive, Daisy Overend saw her garters lying there.

'Put those away,' she commanded Miss Rilke.

The Admiral came first. I opened the door, while with swift and practised skill Daisy and Lotti began a lively conversation, in the midst of which the Admiral was intended to come upon them. Behind the Admiral came a Member of Parliament. They had never been to the house before, not being among Daisy's 'basics'.

'Do come in,' said Miss Rilke, holding open the folding doors.

'This way,' said Tom Pfeffer from the drawing-room.

The two guests stared at the table. Daisy's garters were still there. The Admiral, I could see, was puzzled. Not knowing Daisy very well, he thought, no doubt, she was eccentric. He tried to smile. The political man took rather longer to decide on an attitude. He must have concluded that the garters were not Daisy's, for next I saw him looking curiously at me.

'They are not mine,' I rapidly said, 'those garters.'

'Whose are they?' said the Admiral, drawing near.

'They are Mrs. Overend's garters,' I said, 'she changed her stockings in here.'

Now the garters had never really been serviceable; even now, with the help of safety pins, they did not so much keep Daisy's stockings, as her spirits up, for she liked them. They were historic in the sense that they had at first, I suppose, looked merely naughty. In about five years they had entered their most interesting, their old-fashioned, their lewd period. A little while, and the rosettes had begun to fray: the decadence. And now, with the impurity of those to whom all things pertaining to themselves are pure, Daisy did not see them as junk, but as part of herself, as she had cause to tell me later.

The Admiral walked warily into the drawing-room, but the Member of Parliament lingered to examine a picture on the wall, one eye on the garters. I was, I must say, tempted to hide them somewhere out of sight. More people were arriving, and the garters were causing them to think. If only for this reason, it was perhaps inhospitable to leave them so prominently on the table.

I resisted the temptation. Miss Rilke had suddenly become very excited. She flew to open the door to each guest, and, copying my tone, exclaimed:

'Please to excuse the garters. They are the garters of Mrs. Overend. She changed her stockings in here.'

Daisy, Daisy Overend! I hope you have forgotten me. The party got out of hand. Lotti was not long in leaving the relatively sedative drawing-room in favour of the little room where Daisy's old basics were foregathered. These erstwhile adherents to the Young Idea, arriving in twos and threes, were filled with a great joy on hearing Miss Rilke's speech:

'Please to excuse those garters which you see. They are the garters of Mrs. Overend. . . .'

But there was none more delighted than Lotti.

It was some minutes before the commotion was heard by Daisy in the drawing-room, where she was soliciting the badwill of a journalist against Mr. Jamieson. Meanwhile, the ante-room party joined hands, clinked glasses and danced round Lotti who held the garters aloft with a pair of sugar tongs. Tom Pfeffer so far forgot himself as to curl up with mirth on a sofa.

I remember Daisy as she stood between the folding doors in her black party dress, like an infolded undernourished tulip. Behind her clustered her new friends, slightly offended, though prepared to join in the spirit of the thing, whatever it should be. Before her pranced the old, led by Lotti in a primitive mountain jig. The sugar tongs with the garters in their jaws Lotti held high in one hand, and with the other he plucked the knee of his trouser-leg as if it were a skirt.

'*Ai, Ai, Ai,*' chanted Lotti, 'Daisy's dirty old garters, *Ai!*'

'*Ai, Ai, Ai,*' responded the chorus, while Miss Rilke looked lovingly on, holding in one hand Lotti's drink, in the other her own.

I remember Daisy as she stood there, not altogether without charm, beside herself. While laughter rebounded like plunging breakers from her mouth, she guided her eyes towards myself and trained on me the missiles of her fury. For a full three minutes Daisy's mouth continued to laugh.

148

Daisy Overend

I am seldom in the West End of London. But sometimes I have to hurry across the Piccadilly end of Albemarle Street where the buses crash past like giant orgulous parakeets, more thunderous and more hectic than the Household Cavalry. The shops are on my left and the Green Park lies on my right under the broad countenance of drowsy summer. It is then that, in my mind's eye, Daisy Overend gads again, diminutive, charming, vicious, and tarted up to the nines.

By district messenger she sent me a note early on the morning after the party. I was to come no more. Herewith a cheque. The garters were part of herself and I would understand how she felt.

The cheque was a dud. I did not pursue the matter, and in fact I have forgotten the real name of Daisy Overend. I have forgotten her name but I shall remember it at the Bar of Judgment.

You Should Have Seen
the Mess

I AM now more than glad that I did not pass into the Grammar School five years ago, although it was a disappointment at the time. I was always good at English, but not so good at the other subjects!!

I am glad that I went to the Secondary Modern School, because it was only constructed the year before. Therefore, it was much more hygienic than the Grammar School. The Secondary Modern was light and airy, and the walls were painted with a bright, washable, gloss. One day, I was sent over to the Grammar School, with a note for one of the teachers, and you should have seen the mess! The corridors were dusty, and I saw dust on the window ledges, which were chipped. I saw into one of the classrooms. It was very untidy in there.

I am also glad that I did not go to the Grammar School, because of what it does to one's habits. This may appear to be a strange remark, at first sight. It is a good thing to have an education behind you, and I do not believe in ignorance, but I have had certain experiences, with educated people, since going out into the world.

I am seventeen years of age, and left school two years ago last month. I had my A certificate for typing, so got my first job, as a junior, in a solicitor's office. Mum was pleased at this, and Dad said it was a first-class start, as it was an old established firm. I must say that when I went for the interview, I was surprised at the windows, and the stairs up to the offices were also far from clean. There was a little waiting room, where some of the elements were missing from the gas fire, and the carpet on the floor was worn. However, Mr. Heygate's office, into which I was shown for the interview, was better. The furniture was old, but it was polished, and there was a good carpet, I will say that. The glass of the bookcase was very clean.

I was to start on the Monday, so along I went. They took me to the general office, where there were two senior shorthand-typists, and a clerk, Mr. Gresham, who was far from smart in appearance. You should have seen the mess!! There was no floor covering whatsoever, and so dusty everywhere. There were shelves all round the room, with old box files on them. The box files were falling to pieces, and all the old papers inside them were crumpled. The worst shock of all was the tea cups. It was my duty to make tea, mornings and afternoons. Miss Bewlay showed me where everything was kept. It was kept in an old orange box, and the cups were all cracked. There were not enough saucers to go round, etc. I will not go into the facilities, but they were also far from hygienic. After three days, I told Mum, and she was upset, most of all about the cracked cups. We never keep a cracked cup, but throw it out, because those cracks can harbour germs. So Mum gave me my own cup to take to the office.

Then at the end of the week, when I got my salary,

Mr. Heygate said, 'Well, Lorna, what are you going to do with your first pay?' I did not like him saying this, and I nearly passed a comment, but I said, 'I don't know.' He said, 'What do you do in the evenings, Lorna? Do you watch Telly?' I did take this as an insult, because we call it TV, and his remark made me out to be uneducated. I just stood, and did not answer, and he looked surprised. Next day, Saturday, I told Mum and Dad about the facilities, and we decided I should not go back to that job. Also, the desks in the general office were rickety. Dad was indignant, because Mr. Heygate's concern was flourishing, and he had letters after his name.

Everyone admires our flat, because Mum keeps it spotless, and Dad keeps doing things to it. He has done it up all over, and got permission from the Council to re-modernise the kitchen. I well recall the Health Visitor, remarking to Mum, 'You could eat off your floor, Mrs. Merrifield.' It is true that you could eat your lunch off Mum's floors, and any hour of the day or night you will find every corner spick and span.

Next, I was sent by the agency to a Publisher's for an interview, because of being good at English. One look was enough!! My next interview was a success, and I am still at Low's Chemical Co. It is a modern block, with a quarter of an hour rest period, morning and afternoon. Mr. Marwood is very smart in appearance. He is well spoken, although he has not got a university education behind him. There is special lighting over the desks, and the typewriters are latest models.

So I am happy at Low's. But I have met other

people, of an educated type, in the past year, and it has
opened my eyes. It so happened that I had to go to the
Doctor's house, to fetch a prescription for my young
brother, Trevor, when the epidemic was on. I rang the
bell, and Mrs. Darby came to the door. She was small,
with fair hair, but too long, and a green maternity
dress. But she was very nice to me. I had to wait in
their living-room, and you should have seen the state
it was in! There were broken toys on the carpet, and
the ash trays were full up. There were contemporary
pictures on the walls, but the furniture was not contemporary, but old-fashioned, with covers which were
past standing up to another wash, I should say. To cut
a long story short, Dr. Darby and Mrs. Darby have
always been very kind to me, and they meant everything for the best. Dr. Darby is also short and fair,
and they have three children, a girl and a boy, and now
a baby boy.

When I went that day for the prescription, Dr.
Darby said to me, 'You look pale, Lorna. It's the
London atmosphere. Come on a picnic with us, in the
car, on Saturday.' After that I went with the Darbys
more and more. I liked them, but I did not like the
mess, and it was a surprise. But I also kept in with
them for the opportunity of meeting people, and Mum
and Dad were pleased that I had made nice friends. So
I did not say anything about the cracked lino, and the
paintwork all chipped. The children's clothes were
very shabby for a Doctor, and she changed them out
of their school clothes when they came home from
school, into those worn-out garments. Mum always
kept us spotless to go out to play, and I do not like
to say it, but those Darby children frequently looked

like the Leary family, which the Council evicted from our block, as they were far from houseproud.

One day, when I was there, Mavis (as I called Mrs. Darby by then) put her head out of the window, and shouted to the boy, 'John, stop peeing over the cabbages at once. Pee on the lawn.' I did not know which way to look. Mum would never say a word like that from the window, and I know for a fact that Trevor would never pass water outside, not even bathing in the sea.

I went there usually at the weekends, but sometimes on weekdays, after supper. They had an idea to make a match for me with a chemist's assistant, whom they had taken up too. He was an orphan, and I do not say there was anything wrong with that. But he was not accustomed to those little extras that I was. He was a good-looking boy, I will say that. So I went once to a dance, and twice to the films with him. To look at, he was quite clean in appearance. But there was only hot water at the weekend at his place, and he said that a bath once a week was sufficient. Jim (as I called Dr. Darby by then) said it was sufficient also, and surprised me. He did not have much money, and I do not hold that against him. But there was no hurry for me, and I could wait for a man in a better position, so that I would not miss those little extras. So he started going out with a girl from the coffee bar, and did not come to the Darbys very much then.

There were plenty of boys at the office, but I will say this for the Darbys, they had lots of friends coming and going, and they had interesting conversation, although sometimes it gave me a surprise, and I did not know where to look. And sometimes they had people who were very down and out, although there is no need to be. But most of the guests were different, so it made a comparison with the boys at the office, who were not so educated in their conversation.

Now it was near the time for Mavis to have her baby, and I was to come in at the weekend, to keep an eye on the children, while the help had her day off. Mavis did not go away to have her baby, but would have it at home, in their double bed, as they did not have twin beds, although he was a Doctor. A girl I knew, in our block, was engaged, but was let down, and even she had her baby in the labour ward. I was sure the bedroom was not hygienic for having a baby, but I did not mention it.

One day, after the baby boy came along, they took me in the car to the country, to see Jim's mother. The baby was put in a carry-cot at the back of the car. He began to cry, and without a word of a lie, Jim said to him over his shoulder, 'Oh shut your gob, you little bastard.' I did not know what to do, and Mavis was smoking a cigarette. Dad would not dream of saying such a thing to Trevor or I. When we arrived at Jim's mother's place, Jim said, 'It's a fourteenth-century cottage, Lorna.' I could well believe it. It was very cracked and old, and it made one wonder how Jim could let his old mother live in this tumble-down cottage, as he was so good to everyone else. So Mavis knocked at the door, and the old lady came. There was not much anyone could do to the inside. Mavis said, 'Isn't it charming, Lorna?' If that was a joke, it was going too far. I said to the old Mrs. Darby, 'Are you going to be re-housed?' but she did not understand this, and I explained how you have to apply to the Council, and keep at them. But it was funny that the Council had not done something already, when they go round condemning. Then old Mrs. Darby said, 'My dear, I shall be re-housed in the Grave.' I did not know where to look.

There was a carpet hanging on the wall, which I think was there to hide a damp spot. She had a good TV set, I will say that. But some of the walls were bare brick, and the facilities were outside, through the garden. The furniture was far from new.

One Saturday afternoon, as I happened to go to the Darbys, they were just going off to a film, and they took me too. It was the Curzon, and afterwards we went to a flat in Curzon Street. It was a very clean block, I will say that, and there were good carpets at the entrance. The couple there had contemporary furniture, and they also spoke about music. It was a nice place, but there was no Welfare Centre to the flats, where people could go for social intercourse, advice and guidance. But they were well-spoken, and I met Willy Morley, who was an artist. Willy sat beside me, and we had a drink. He was young, dark, with a dark shirt, so one could not see right away if he was clean. Soon after this, Jim said to me, 'Willy wants to paint you, Lorna. But you'd better ask your Mum.' Mum said it was all right if he was a friend of the Darbys.

I can honestly say that Willy's place was the most unhygienic place I have seen in my life. He said I had an unusual type of beauty, which he must capture. This was when we came back to his place from the restaurant. The light was very dim, but I could see the bed had not been made, and the sheets were far from clean. He said he must paint me, but I told Mavis I did not like to go back there. 'Don't you like Willy?' she asked. I could not deny that I liked Willy, in a way. There was something about him, I will say that. Mavis said, 'I hope he hasn't been making a pass at you, Lorna.' I said he had not done so, which was almost true, because he did not attempt to go to the full extent. It was always unhygienic when I went to Willy's place, and I told him so once, but he said, 'Lorna, you are a joy.' He had a nice way, and he took me out in his car, which was a good one, but dirty inside, like his place. Jim said one day, 'He has pots of money, Lorna,' and Mavis said, 'You might make a man of him, as he is keen on you.' They always said Willy came from a good family.

But I saw that one could not do anything with him. He would not change his shirt very often, or get clothes, but he went round like a tramp, lending people money, as I have seen with my own eyes. His place was in a terrible mess, with the empty bottles, and laundry in the corner. He gave me several gifts over the period, which I took, as he would have only given them away, but he never tried to go to the full extent. He never painted my portrait, as he was painting fruit on a table all that time, and they said his pictures were marvellous, and thought Willy and I were getting married.

One night, when I went home, I was upset as usual, after Willy's place. Mum and Dad had gone to bed, and I looked round our kitchen which is done in primrose and white. Then I went into the living-room, where Dad has done one wall in a patterned paper, deep rose and white, and the other walls pale rose, with white wood-work. The suite is new, and Mum keeps everything beautiful. So it came to me, all of a sudden, what a fool I was, going with Willy. I agree to equality, but as to me marrying Willy, as I said to Mavis, when I recall his place, and the good carpet gone greasy, not to mention the paint oozing out of the tubes, I think it would break my heart to sink so low.

Come Along, Marjorie

NOT many days had passed since my arrival at Watling Abbey when I realised that most of us were recovering from nerves. The Abbey, a twelfth-century foundation, lies in Worcestershire on the site of an ancient Temple of Mithras. It had recently been acquired and restored by its original religious Order at that time, just after the war, when I went to stay there and found after a few days that most of us were nervous cases.

By 'most of us' I mean the lay visitors who resided in the pilgrims' quarters on two sides of the Annexe. We were all known as pilgrims. Apart from us, there was a group of permanent lay residents known as the Cloisters, because they lived in rooms above the cloisters.

Neurotics are awfully quick to notice other people's mentalities, everyone goes into an exaggerated category. I placed four categories at the Abbey. First ourselves, the visiting neurotic pilgrims. Second the Cloisters, they were cranks on the whole. Third the monks; they seemed not to have nerves, but non-individualized, non-neurotic, so I thought then, they billowed about in their white habits under the gold of that October, or swung out from the cloisters in processions on Feast Days. Into the fourth category I placed Miss Marjorie Pettigrew.

Indeed, she did seem sane. I got the instant impression that she alone among the lay people, both pilgrims and Cloisters, understood the purpose of the place. I did get that impression.

Three of us had arrived at Watling together. It was dark when I got off the train, but under the only gas bracket on the platform I saw the two women standing. They looked about them in that silly manner of women unused to arriving at strange railway stations. They heard me asking the ticket man the way to the Abbey and chummed up with me immediately. As we walked along with our suitcases I made note that there was little in common between them and me except Catholicism, and then only in the mystical sense, for their religious apprehensions were different from mine. 'Different from' is the form my neurosis takes. I do like the differentiation of things, but it is apt to lead to nerve-racking pursuits. On the other hand, life led on the different-from level is always an adventure.

Those were quite nice women. One was Squackle-wackle, so I called her to myself, for she spoke like that, squackle-wackle, squackle-wackle — it was her neurosis — all about her job as a nurse in a London hospital. She had never managed to pass an exam but was content, squackle-wackle, to remain a subordinate, though thirty-three in December. All this in the first four minutes. The other woman would be nearer forty. She was quieter, but not much. As we approached the Abbey gates she said, 'My name's Jennifer, what's yours?'

'Gloria Deplores-you,' I answered. It is true my Christian name is Gloria.

'Gloria what?'

'It's a French name,' I said, inventing in my mind the spelling 'des Pleuresyeux' in case I should be pressed for it.

'We'll call you Gloria,' she said. I had stopped in the Abbey gateway, wondering if I should turn back after all. 'Come along, Gloria,' she said.

It was not till some days later that I found that Jennifer's neurosis took the form of 'same as'. We are all the same, she would assert, infuriating me because I knew that God had made everyone unique. 'We are all the same' was her way of saying we were all equal in the sight of God. Still, the inaccuracy irritated me. And still, like Squackle-wackle, she was quite an interesting person. It was only in my more vibrant moments that I deplored them.

Oh, the trifles, the people, that get on your nerves when you have a neurosis!

Don't I remember the little ginger man with the bottle-green cloak? He was one of the Cloisters, having been resident at Watling for over three years. He was compiling a work called *The Monkish Booke of Brewes*. Once every fortnight he would be absent at the British Museum and I suppose other record houses, from where he would return with a great pad of notes on the methods and subtleties of brewing practised in ancient monasteries, don't I remember? And he, too, was a kindly sort in between his frightful fumes against the management of Watling Abbey. When anything went wrong he blamed the monks, unlike the Irish who blamed the Devil. This sometimes caused friction between the ginger man and the Irish, for which the monks blamed the Devil.

There were ladies from Cork and thereabouts, ladies from Tyrone and Londonderry, all having come for a rest or a Retreat, and most bearing those neurotic stigmata of South or North accordingly. There were times when bitter bits of meaning would whistle across the space between North and South when they were gathered together outside of their common worship. Though all were Catholics, 'Temperament tells,' I told myself frequently. I did so often tell myself remarks like that to still my own nerves.

I joined Squackle-wackle and Jennifer each morning to recite the Fifteen Mysteries. After that we went to the town for coffee. Because I rested in the afternoons Jennifer guessed I was recovering from nerves. She asked me outright, 'Is it nerves?' I said 'Yes,' outright.

Squackle-wackle had also been sent away with nervous exhaustion, she made no secret of it, indeed no.

Jennifer was delighted. 'I've got the same trouble. Fancy, all three of us. That makes us *all the same*.'

'It makes us,' I said, 'more different from each other than other people are.'

'But, all the same,' she said, 'we're all *the same*.'

But there was Miss Marjorie Pettigrew. Miss Pettigrew's appearance and bearing attracted me with a kind of consolation. I learned that she had been at Watling for about six months and from various hints and abrupt silences I gathered that she was either feared or disliked. I put this down to the fact that she wasn't a neurotic. Usually, neurotics take against people whose nerves they can't jar upon. So I argued to myself; and that I myself rather approved of Miss

Pettigrew was a sign that I was a different sort of neurotic from the others.

Miss Pettigrew was very tall and stick-like, with very high shoulders and a square face. She seemed to have a lot of bones. Her eyes were dark, her hair black; it was coiled in the earphone style but she was not otherwise unfashionable.

I thought at first she must be in Retreat, for she never spoke at mealtimes, though she always smiled faintly when passing anything at table. She never joined the rest of the community except for meals and prayers. She was often in the chapel praying. I envied her resistance, for though I too wanted solitude I often hadn't the courage to refuse to join the company, and so make myself unpopular like Miss Pettigrew. I hoped she would speak to me when she came out of her Retreat.

One day in that first week a grand-looking north-countrywoman said to me at table, nodding over to where Miss Pettigrew sat in her silence,

'There's nothing wrong with *her* at all.'

'Wrong with her?'

'It's pretence, she's clever, that's it.'

By clever she meant cunning, I realised that much.

'How do you mean, pretence?' I said.

'Her silence. She won't speak to anyone.'

'But she's in Retreat, isn't she?'

'Not her,' said this smart woman. 'She's been living here for over six months and for the past four she hasn't opened her mouth. It isn't mental trouble, it is not.'

'Has she taken some religious vow, perhaps?'

'Not her; she's clever. She won't open her mouth.

They brought a doctor, but she wouldn't open her mouth to him.'

'I'm glad she's quiet, anyhow,' I said. 'Her room's next door to mine and I like quietness.'

Not all the pilgrims regarded Miss Pettigrew as 'clever'. She was thought to be genuinely touched in the head. And it was strange how she was disapproved of by the Cloisters, for they were kind — only too intrusively kind — towards obvious nervous sufferers like me. Their disapproval of Miss Pettigrew was almost an admission that they believed nothing wrong with her. If she had gone untidy, made grotesque faces, given jerks and starts and twitches, if she had in some way lost their respect I do not think she would have lost their approval.

I began to notice her more closely in the hope of finding out more about her mental aberration; such things are like a magnet to neurotics. I would meet her crossing the courtyard, or come upon her kneeling in the lonely Lady Chapel. Always she inclined her coiled head towards me, ceremonious as an Abbess greeting a nun. Passing her in a corridor I felt the need to stand aside and make way for her confident quiet progress. I could not believe she was insane.

I could not believe she was practising some crude triumphant cunning, enduring from day to day, with her silence and prayers. It was said she had money. Perhaps she was very mystical. I wondered how long she would be able to remain hermitted so within herself. The monks were in a difficult position. It was against their nature to turn her out; maybe it was against their Rule; certainly it would cause a bad impression in the neighbourhood which was not at all Abbey-minded. One after another the monks had approached her, tactful monks, sympathetic, firm and curious ones.

'Well, Miss Pettigrew, I hope you've benefited from your stay at the Abbey? I suppose you have plans for the winter?'

No answer, only a mild gesture of acknowledgment.

No answer, likewise, to another monk, 'Now, Miss Pettigrew, dear child, you simply can't go on like this. It isn't that we don't want to keep you. Glory be to God, we'd never turn you out of doors, nor any soul. But we need the room, d'you see, for another pilgrim.'

And again, 'Now tell us what's the trouble, open your heart, poor Miss Pettigrew. This isn't the Catholic way at all. You've got to communicate with your fellows.'

'Is it a religious vow you've taken all on your own? That's very unwise, it's . . .'

'See, Miss Pettigrew, we've found you a lodging in the town . . .'

Not a word. She was seen to go weekly to Confession, so evidently she was capable of speech. But she would not talk, even to do her small bits of shopping. Every week or so she would write on a piece of paper,

'Please get me a Snowdrop Shampoo, 1/6d. encl.' or some such errand, handing it to the laundry-girl who was much attached to her, and who showed me these slips of paper as proudly as if they were the relics of a saint.

'Gloria, are you coming for a walk?'

No, I wasn't going for a trudge. It was my third week. Squackle-wackle was becoming most uninteresting.

I sat by my window and thought how happy I would be if I wasn't waiting uncertainly for a telephone call. I still have in mind the blue and green and gold of that October afternoon which was spoiled for me at the time. The small ginger man with his dark green cloak slipping off his shoulders crossed the grass in the courtyard below. Two lay brothers in blue workmen's overalls were manipulating a tractor away in the distance. From the Lady Chapel came the chant of the monks at their office. There is nothing like plainsong to eternalise a memory, it puts a seal on whatever is happening at the time. I thought it a pity that my appreciation of this fact should be vitiated by an overwhelming need for the telephone call.

I had hoped, in fact, that the ginger man had crossed the courtyard to summon me to the telephone, but he disappeared beneath my window and his footsteps faded out somewhere round the back. Everything's perfect, I told myself, and I can't enjoy it. Brown, white and purple, I distinguished the pigeons on the grass.

Everyone else seemed to be out of doors. My room was on the attic floor, under the dusty beams of the roof. All along this top floor the rooms were separated by thin partitions which allowed transit to every sound. Even silent Miss Pettigrew, my immediate neighbour, could not lie breathing on her still bed without my knowing it. That afternoon she too was out, probably over in the chapel.

The telephone call was to be from Jonathan, my very best friend. I had returned from my coffee session in the town that morning to find a letter from him which had been delayed in the post. 'I'll ring you at 11.30,' he had written, referring to that very day. It was then past twelve. At eleven-thirty I had been drinking coffee with unutterable Squackle-wackle and Jennifer.

'Has there been a call for me?' I enquired.

'Not that I know,' said the secretary vaguely. 'I've been away from the phone all morning of course, so there may have been, I don't know.'

Not that there was anything important to discuss with Jonathan; the idea was only to have a chat. But at that moment I felt imperatively dependent on his voice over the telephone. I stopped everyone, monks and brothers and pilgrims. 'Did you take a telephone message for me? I should have received a very urgent call. It should have come at eleven-thirty.'

'Sorry, I've been out,' or 'Sorry, I haven't been near the phone.'

'Doesn't anyone attend to your telephone?' I demanded.

'Hardly ever, dear. We're too busy.'

'I've missed an important telephone call, a vital——'

'Can't you telephone to your friend from here?'

'No,' I said. 'It's impossible, it's too bad.'

Jonathan did not have a telephone in his studio. I wondered whether I should send him a wire and even drafted one, 'Sorry love your letter arrived too late was out please ring at once love Gloria.' I tore this up on the grounds that I couldn't afford the expense. And something about the torment of the affair attracted me, it was better than boredom. I decided that Jonathan would surely ring again during the afternoon. I prepared, even, to sit in the little office by the telephone with my sense of suspense and vigilance, all afternoon. But, 'I'll be here till five o'clock,' said the secretary;

'of course, of course, I'll send for you if the call comes.'

And so there I was by the window waiting for the summons. At three o'clock I washed and made up my face and changed my frock as if this were a propitiation to whatever stood between Jonathan's telephone call and me. I decided to stroll round the green-gold court-yard where I could not fail to miss any messenger. Once round, and still no-one came. Only Miss Pettigrew emerged from the cloisters, crossing the courtyard towards me.

I was so bemused by my need to talk to Jonathan that I thought, as she approached, 'Perhaps they've sent her to call me.' Immediately I remembered, that was absurd, for she carried no messages ever. But she continued so directly towards me that I thought again, 'She's going to speak.' She had her dark eyes on my face.

I made as if to pass her, not wishing to upset her by inviting approach. But she stopped me. 'Excuse me,' she said, 'I have a message for you.'

I was so relieved that I forgot to be surprised by her speaking.

'Am I wanted on the telephone?' I said, half-ready to run across to the office.

'No, I have a message for you,' she said.

'What's the message?'

'The Lord is risen,' she said.

It was not until I had got over my disappointment that I felt the shock of her having spoken, and recalled an odd focus of her eyes that I had not seen before. 'After all,' I thought, 'she has a religious mania. She *is* different from the neurotics, but not because she is sane.'

'Gloria!' — this was the girl from the repository poking her head round the door. She beckoned to me, and, still disturbed, I idled over to her.

'I say, did I see Miss Pettigrew actually speaking to you, or was I dreaming?'

'You were dreaming.' If I had said otherwise the news would have bristled round the monastery. It would have seemed a betrayal to reveal this first crack in Miss Pettigrew's control. The pilgrims would have pitied her more if they had known of it, they would have respected her less. I could not bear to think of their heads shaking sorrowfully over Miss Pettigrew's vital 'The Lord is risen.'

'But surely,' this girl pursued, 'she stopped beside you just now.'

'You've got Miss Pettigrew on the brain,' I said. 'Leave her alone, poor soul.'

'Poor soul!' said the girl. 'I don't know about poor soul. There's nothing wrong with that one. She's got foolish medieval ideas, that's all.'

'There's nothing to be done with her,' I said.

And yet it was not long before something had to be done with Miss Pettigrew. From the Sunday of the fourth week of my stay she went off food. It was not till supper-time on the Monday that her absence was noticed from the refectory.

'Anyone seen Miss Pettigrew?'

'No, she hasn't been down here for two days.'

'Does she eat in the town, perhaps?'

'No, she hasn't left the Abbey.'

A deputation with a tray of food was sent to her room. There was no answer. The door was bolted

from the inside. But I heard her moving calmly as
ever in her room that evening.

Next morning she came in to breakfast after Mass,
looking distant and grey, but still very neat. She took
up a glass of milk, lifted the crust end of the bread from
the board and carried them shakily off to her room.
When she did not appear for lunch the cook tried her
room again, without success. The door was bolted,
there was no answer.

I saw Miss Pettigrew again at Mass next morning,
kneeling a little in front of me, resting her head upon her
missal as if she could not bear the weight of head on
neck. When at last she left the chapel she walked
extremely slowly but without halting in her measure.
Squackle-wackle ran to help her down the steps. Miss
Pettigrew stopped and looked at her, inclining her head
in recognition, but clearly rejecting her help.

The doctor was waiting in her room. I heard later
that he asked her many questions, used many per-
suasives, but she simply stared right through him. The
Abbot and several of the monks visited her, but by then
she had bolted the door again, and though they tempted
her with soups and beef broth, Miss Pettigrew would
not open.

News went round that her relatives had been sent for.
The news went round that she had no relatives to send
for. It was said she had been certified insane and was
to be taken away.

She did not rise next morning at her usual seven
o'clock. It was not till after twelve that I heard her
first movement, and the protracted sounds of her slow
rising and dressing. A tiny clatter — that would be her
shoe falling out of her weak hands; I knew she was

bending down, trying again. My pulse was pattering so rapidly that I had to take more of my sedative than usual, as I listened to this slow deliberated performance. Heavy rhythmic rain had started to ping on the roof.

'Neurotics never go mad,' my friends had always told me. Now I realised the distinction between neurosis and madness, and in my agitation I half-envied the woman beyond my bedroom wall, the sheer cool sanity of her behaviour within the limits of her impracticable mania. Only the very mad, I thought, can come out with the information 'The Lord is risen', in the same factual way as one might say, 'You are wanted on the telephone', regardless of the time and place.

A knock at my door. I opened it, still shaking with my nerves. It was Jennifer. She whispered, with an eye on the partition dividing me from Miss Pettigrew,

'Come along, Gloria. They say you are to come away for half an hour. The nurses are coming to fetch *her*.'

'What nurses?'

'From the asylum. And there will be men with a stretcher. We haven't to distress ourselves, they say.'

I could see that Jennifer was agog. She was more transparent than I was. I could see she was longing to stay and overhear, watch out of the windows, see what would happen. I was overcome with disgust and indignation. Why should Jennifer want to satisfy her curiosity? She believed everyone was 'the same', she didn't acknowledge the difference of things, what right had she to possess curiosity? My case was different.

'I shall stay here,' I said in a normal voice, signifying that I wasn't going to participate in any whispering. Jennifer disappeared, annoyed.

Insanity was my great sort of enemy at that time. And here, clothed in the innocence and dignity of Miss Pettigrew, was my next-door enemy being removed by ambulance. I would not miss it. Afterwards I learned that Jennifer too was lurking around when the ambulance arrived. So were most of the neurotics.

The ambulance came round the back. My window looked only on the front but my ears were windows. I heard a woman's voice, then in reply the voice of one of our priests. Heavy footsteps and something bumping on the stairs, and strange men's voices ascending.

'What's her name, did you say?'

'Marjorie Pettigrew.'

The hauling and bumping up the stairs continued.

'Ain't no key. Bolt from the inside.'

Whenever they paused I could hear Miss Pettigrew's tiny movements. She was continuing to do what she was doing.

They knocked at the door. I pulled like mad at the Rosary which I was telling for Miss Pettigrew. A man's voice said, kindly but terribly loud,

'Open up the door, dear. Else we shall have to force it, dear.'

She opened the door.

'That's a good girl,' said the man. 'What was the name again?'

The other man replied, 'Marjorie Pettigrew.'

'Well, come on, Marjorie dear. You just follow me and you won't go wrong. Come along, Marjorie.'

I knew she must have been following, though I could not hear her footsteps. I heard the heavy men's boots descending the stairs, and their unnecessary equipment bumping behind them.

'That's right, Marjorie. That's a good girl.'

Down below the nurse said something, and I heard no more till the ambulance drove off.

'Oh, I saw her!' This was the laundry-girl who had been fond of Miss Pettigrew. 'She must have been combing her hair,' she said, 'when they came for her. It was all loose and long, not at all like Miss Pettigrew. She was always just so. And that going out in the rain, I hope she doesn't catch cold. But they'll be good to her.'

Everyone was saying, 'They will be kind to her.' 'They will look after her.' 'They might cure her.'

I never saw them so friendly with each other.

After supper someone said, 'I had a respect for Miss Pettigrew.'

'So did I,' said another.

'Yes, so did I.'

'They will very be kind. Those men — they sounded all right.'

'They meant well enough.'

Suddenly the ginger man came out with that one thing which stood at the core of this circuitous talk.

'Did you hear them,' he said, 'calling her Marjorie?'

'My God, yes!'

'Yes, it made me feel funny.'

'Same here. Fancy calling her Marjorie.'

After that the incident was little discussed. But the community was sobered and united for a brief time, contemplating with fear and pity the calling of Miss Pettigrew Marjorie.

The Seraph and the Zambesi

You may have heard of Samuel Cramer, half poet, half journalist, who had to do with a dancer called the Fanfarlo. But, as you will see, it doesn't matter if you have not. He was said to be going strong in Paris early in the nineteenth century, and when I met him in 1946 he was still going strong, but this time in a different way. He was the same man, but modified. For instance, in those days, more than a hundred years ago, Cramer had persisted for several decades, and without affectation, in being about twenty-five years old. But when I knew him he was clearly undergoing his forty-two-year-old phase.

At this time he was keeping a petrol pump some four miles south of the Zambesi River where it crashes over a precipice at the Victoria Falls. Cramer had some spare rooms where he put up visitors to the Falls when the hotel was full. I was sent to him because it was Christmas week and there was no room in the hotel.

I found him trying the starter of a large, lumpy Mercedes outside his corrugated-iron garage, and at first sight I judged him to be a Belgian from the Congo. He had the look of north and south, light hair with canvas-coloured skin. Later, however, he told me that his father was German and his mother Chilean. It was this information rather than the 'S. Cramer' above the garage door which made me think I had heard of him.

The rains had been very poor and that December was fiercely hot. On the third night before Christmas I sat on the stoep outside my room, looking through the broken mosquito-wire network at the lightning in the distance. When an atmosphere maintains an excessive temperature for a long spell something seems to happen to the natural noises of life. Sound fails to carry in its usual quantity, but comes as if bound and gagged. That night the Christmas beetles, which fall on their backs on every stoep with a high tic-tac, seemed to be shock-absorbed. I saw one fall and the little bump reached my ears a fraction behind-time. The noises of minor wild beasts from the bush were all hushed-up, too. In fact it wasn't until the bush noises all stopped simultaneously, as they frequently do when a leopard is about, that I knew there had been any sound at all.

Overlying this general muted hum, Cramer's sun-downer party progressed farther up the stoep. The heat distorted every word. The glasses made a tinkle that was not of the substance of glass, but of bottles wrapped in tissue paper. Sometimes, for a moment, a shriek or a cackle would hang torpidly in space, but these were unreal sounds, as if projected from a distant country, as if they were pocket-torches seen through a London fog.

Cramer came over to my end of the stoep and asked me to join his party. I said I would be glad to, and meant it, even though I had been glad to sit alone. Heat so persistent and so intense sucks up the will.

Five people sat in wicker arm-chairs drinking high-balls and chewing salted peanuts. I recognised a red-haired trooper from Livingstone, just out from England, and two of Cramer's lodgers, a tobacco planter and his wife from Bulawayo. In the custom of those parts, the other two were introduced by their first names. Mannie, a short dark man of square face and build, I thought might be a Portuguese from the east coast. The woman, Fanny, was picking bits out of the frayed wicker chair and as she lifted her glass her hand shook a little, making her bracelets chime. She would be about fifty, a well-tended woman, very neat. Her grey hair, tinted with blue, was done in a fringe above a face puckered with malaria.

In the general way of passing the time with strangers in that countryside, I exchanged with the tobacco people the names of acquaintances who lived within a six-hundred-mile radius of where we sat, reducing this list to names mutually known to us. The trooper contributed his news from the region between Lusaka and Livingstone. Meanwhile an argument was in process between Cramer, Fanny and Mannie, of which Fanny seemed to be getting the better. It appeared there was to be a play or concert on Christmas Eve in which the three were taking part. I several times heard the words 'troupe of angels', 'shepherds', 'ridiculous price' and 'my girls' which seemed to be key words in the argument. Suddenly, on hearing the trooper mention a name, Fanny broke off her talk and turned to us.

'She was one of my girls,' she said, 'I gave her lessons for three years.'

Mannie rose to leave, and before Fanny followed him she picked a card from her handbag and held it out to me between her fingernails.

'If any of your friends are interested . . .' said Fanny hazily.

I looked at this as she drove off with the man, and above an address about four miles up the river I read:

The Seraph and the Zambesi

Mme La Fanfarlo (Paris, London)
Dancing Instructress. Ballet. Ballroom.
Transport provided By Arrangement.

Next day I came across Cramer still trying to locate the trouble with the Mercedes.

'Are you the man Baudelaire wrote about?' I asked him.

He stared past me at the open waste veldt with a look of tried patience.

'Yes,' he replied. 'What made you think of it?'

'The name Fanfarlo on Fanny's card,' I said. 'Didn't you know her in Paris?'

'Oh, yes,' said Cramer, 'but those days are finished. She married Manuela de Montaverde — that's Mannie. They settled here about twenty years ago. He keeps a Kaffir store.'

I remembered then that in the Romantic age it had pleased Cramer to fluctuate between the practice of verse and that of belles lettres, together with the living up to such practices.

I asked him, 'Have you given up your literary career?'

'*As* a career, yes,' he answered. 'It was an obsession I was glad to get rid of.'

He stroked the blunt bonnet of the Mercedes and added, 'The greatest literature is the occasional kind, a mere afterthought.'

Again he looked across the veldt where, unseen, a grey-crested lourie was piping 'go'way, go'way'.

'Life,' Cramer continued, 'is the important thing.'

'And do you write occasional verses?' I inquired.

'When occasion demands it,' he said. 'In fact I've

just written a Nativity Masque. We're giving a performance on Christmas Eve in there.' He pointed to his garage, where a few natives were already beginning to shift petrol-cans and tyres. Being members neither of the cast nor the audience, they were taking their time. A pile of folded seats had been dumped alongside.

Late on the morning of Christmas Eve I returned from the Falls to find a crowd of natives quarrelling outside the garage, with Cramer swearing loud and heavy in the middle. He held a sulky man by the shirt-sleeve, while with the other hand he described his vituperation on the hot air. Some mission natives had been sent over to give a hand with laying the stage, and these, with their standard-three school English, washed faces and white drill shorts, had innocently provoked Cramer's raw rag-dressed boys. Cramer's method, which ended with the word 'police', succeeded in sending them back to work, still uttering drum-like gutturals at each other.

The stage, made of packing-cases with planks nailed across, was being put at the back of the building, where a door led to the yard, the privy and the native huts. The space between this door and the stage was closed off by a row of black Government blankets hung on a line; this was to be the dressing-room. I agreed to come round there that evening to help with the lighting, the make-up, and the pinning on of angels' wings. The Fanfarlo's dancing pupils were to make an angel chorus with carols and dancing, while she herself, as the Virgin, was to give a representative ballet performance. Owing to her husband's very broken English, he had been given a silent role as a shepherd, supported by three other shepherds chosen for like reasons. Cramer's part was the most prominent, for he had the longest speeches, being the First Seraph. It had been agreed that, since he had written the masque, he could best deliver most of it; but I gathered there had been some trouble at rehearsals over the cost of the production, with Fanny wanting elaborate scenery as being due to her girls.

The performance was set to begin at eight. I arrived behind the stage at seven-fifteen to find the angels assembled in ballet dresses with wings of crinkled paper in various shades. The Fanfarlo wore a long white transparent skirt with a sequin top. I was helping to fix on the Wise Men's beards when I saw Cramer. He had on a toga-like garment made up of several thicknesses of mosquito-net, but not thick enough to hide his white shorts underneath. He had put on his make-up early, and this was melting on his face in the rising heat.

'I always get nerves at this point,' he said. 'I'm going to practise my opening speech.'

I heard him mount the stage and begin reciting. Above the voices of excited children I could only hear the rhythm of his voice; and I was intent on helping the Fanfarlo to paint her girls' faces. It seemed impossible. As fast as we lifted the sticks of paint they turned liquid. It was really getting abnormally hot.

'Open that door,' yelled the Fanfarlo. The back door was opened and a crowd of curious natives pressed round the entrance. I left the Fanfarlo ordering them off, for I was determined to get to the front of the build-ing for some air. I mounted the stage and began to cross it when I was aware of a powerful radiation of

heat coming from my right. Looking round, I saw
Cramer apparently shouting at someone, in the attitude
of his dealings with the natives that morning. But he
could not advance because of this current of heat. And
because of the heat I could not at first make out who
Cramer was rowing with; this was the sort of heat that
goes for the eyes. But as I got further towards the front
of the stage I saw what was standing there.

This was a living body. The most noticeable thing
was its constancy; it seemed not to conform to the law
of perspective, but remained the same size when I
approached as when I withdrew. And altogether unlike other forms of life, it had a completed look. No
part was undergoing a process; the outline lacked the
signs of confusion and ferment which are commonly the
signs of living things, and this was also the principle of
its beauty. The eyes took up nearly the whole of the
head, extending far over the cheekbones. From the
back of the head came two muscular wings which from
time to time folded themselves over the eyes, making a
draught of scorching air. There was hardly any neck.
Another pair of wings, tough and supple, spread from
below the shoulders, and a third pair extended from the
calves of the legs, appearing to sustain the body. The
feet looked too fragile to bear up such a concentrated
degree of being.

European residents of Africa are often irresistibly
prompted to speak Kitchen Kaffir to anything strange.

'*Hamba!*' shouted Cramer, meaning 'Go away'.

'Now get off the stage and stop your noise,' said the
living body peaceably.

'Who in hell are you?' said Cramer, gasping through
the heat.

'The same as in Heaven,' came the reply, 'a Seraph, that's to say.'

'Tell that to someone else,' Cramer panted. 'Do I look like a fool?'

'I will. No, nor a Seraph either,' said the Seraph.

The place was filling with heat from the Seraph. Cramer's paint was running into his eyes and he wiped them on his net robe. Walking backward to a less hot place he cried, 'Once and for all——'

'That's correct,' said the Seraph.

'—— this is my show,' continued Cramer.

'Since when?' the Seraph said.

'Right from the start,' Cramer breathed at him.

'Well, it's been mine from the Beginning,' said the Seraph, 'and the Beginning began first.'

Climbing down from the hot stage, Cramer caught his seraphic robe on a nail and tore it. 'Listen here,' he said, 'I can't conceive of an abnormality like you being a true Seraph.'

'True,' said the Seraph.

By this time I had been driven by the heat to the front entrance. Cramer joined me there. A number of natives had assembled. The audience had begun to arrive in cars and the rest of the cast had come round the building from the back. It was impossible to see far inside the building owing to the Seraph's heat, and impossible to re-enter.

Cramer was still haranguing the Seraph from the door, and there was much speculation amongst the new arrivals as to which of the three familiar categories the present trouble came under, namely, the natives, Whitehall, or leopards.

'This is my property,' cried Cramer, 'and these

people have paid for their seats. They've come to see a masque.'

'In that case,' said the Seraph, 'I'll cool down and they can come and see a masque.'

'*My* masque,' said Cramer.

'Ah, no, *mine*,' said the Seraph. 'Yours won't do.'

'Will you go, or shall I call the police?' said Cramer with finality.

'I have no alternative,' said the Seraph more finally still.

Word had gone round that a mad leopard was in the garage. People got back into their cars and parked at a safe distance; the tobacco planter went to fetch a gun. A number of young troopers had the idea of blinding the mad leopard with petrol and ganged up some natives to fill petrol cans from the pump and pass them chainwise to the garage.

'This'll fix him,' said a trooper.

'That's right, let him have it,' said Cramer from his place by the door.

'I shouldn't do that,' said the Seraph. 'You'll cause a fire.'

The first lot of petrol to be flung into the heat flared up. The seats caught alight first, then the air itself began to burn within the metal walls till the whole interior was flame feeding on flame. Another car-load of troopers arrived just then and promptly got a gang of natives to fill petrol cans with water. Slowly they drenched the fire. The Fanfarlo mustered her angels a little way up the road. She was trying to reassure their parents and see what was happening at the same time, furious at losing her opportunity to dance. She aimed a hard poke at the back of one of the angels whose parents were in England.

It was some hours before the fire was put out. While the corrugated metal walls still glowed, twisted and furled, it was impossible to see what had happened to the Seraph, and after they had ceased to glow it was too dark and hot to see far into the wreck.

'Are you insured?' one of Cramer's friends asked him.

'Oh yes,' Cramer replied, 'my policy covers everything except Acts of God—that means lightning or flood.'

'He's fully covered,' said Cramer's friend to another friend.

Many people had gone home and the rest were going. The troopers drove off singing 'Good King Wenceslas', and the mission boys ran down the road singing 'Good Christian Men, Rejoice'.

It was about midnight, and still very hot. The tobacco planters suggested a drive to the Falls, where it was cool. Cramer and the Fanfarlo joined us, and we bumped along the rough path from Cramer's to the main highway. There the road is tarred only in two strips to take car-wheels. The thunder of the Falls reached us about two miles before we reached them.

'After all my work on the masque and everything!' Cramer was saying.

'Oh, shut up,' said the Fanfarlo.

Just then, by the glare of our headlights I saw the Seraph again, going at about seventy miles an hour and skimming the tarmac strips with two of his six wings in swift motion, two folded over his face, and two covering his feet.

'That's him!' said Cramer. 'We'll get him yet.'

We left the car near the hotel and followed a track through the dense vegetation of the Rain Forest, where the spray from the Falls descends perpetually. It was like a convalescence after fever, that frail rain after the heat. The Seraph was far ahead of us and through the trees I could see where his heat was making steam of the spray.

We came to the cliff's edge, where opposite us and from the same level the full weight of the river came blasting into the gorge between. There was no sign of the Seraph. Was he far below in the heaving pit, or where?

Then I noticed that along the whole mile of the waterfall's crest the spray was rising higher than usual. This I took to be steam from the Seraph's heat. I was right, for presently, by the mute flashes of summer lightning we watched him ride the Zambesi away from us, among the rocks that look like crocodiles and the crocodiles that look like rocks.

The Portobello Road

ONE day in my young youth at high summer, lolling with my lovely companions upon a haystack I found a needle. Already and privately for some years I had been guessing that I was set apart from the common run, but this of the needle attested the fact to my whole public, George, Kathleen and Skinny. I sucked my thumb, for when I had thrust my idle hand deep into the hay, the thumb was where the needle had stuck.

When everyone had recovered George said, 'She put in her thumb and pulled out a plum.' Then away we were into our merciless hacking-hecking laughter again.

The needle had gone fairly deep into the thumby cushion and a small red river flowed and spread from this tiny puncture. So that nothing of our joy should lag, George put in quickly,

'Mind your bloody thumb on my shirt.'

Then hac-hec-hoo, we shrieked into the hot Borderland afternoon. Really I should not care to be so young of heart again. That is my thought every time I turn over my old papers and come across the photograph. Skinny, Kathleen and myself are in the photo atop the haystack. Skinny had just finished analysing the inwards of my find.

'It couldn't have been done by brains. You haven't much brains but you're a lucky wee thing.'

Everyone agreed that the needle betokened extraordinary luck. As it was becoming a serious conversation, George said,

'I'll take a photo.'

I wrapped my hanky round my thumb and got myself organised. George pointed up from his camera and shouted,

'Look, there's a mouse!'

Kathleen screamed and I screamed although I think we knew here was no mouse. But this gave us an extra session of squalling hee-hoo's. Finally we three composed ourselves for George's picture. We look lovely and it was a great day at the time, but I would not care for it all over again. From that day I was known as Needle.

One Saturday in recent years I was mooching down the Portobello Road, threading among the crowds of marketers on the narrow pavement when I saw a woman. She had a haggard careworn wealthy look, thin but for the breasts forced-up high like a pigeon's. I had not seen her for nearly five years. How changed she was! But I recognised Kathleen, my friend; her features had already begun to sink and protrude in the way that mouths and noses do in people destined always to be old for their years. When I had last seen her, nearly five years ago, Kathleen, barely thirty, had said,

'I've lost all my looks, it's in the family. All the women are handsome as girls, but we go off early, we go brown and nosey.'

I stood silently among the people, watching. As you will see, I wasn't in a position to speak to Kathleen. I saw her shoving in her avid manner from stall to stall. She was always fond of antique jewellery and of bargains. I wondered that I had not seen her before in the Portobello Road on my Saturday morning ambles. Her long stiff-crooked fingers pounced to select a jade ring from amongst the jumble of brooches and pendants, onyx, moonstone and gold, set out on the stall.

'What d'you think of this?' she said.

I saw then who was with her. I had been half-conscious of the huge man following several paces behind her, and now I noticed him.

'It looks all right,' he said. 'How much is it?'

'How much is it?' Kathleen asked the vendor.

I took a good look at this man accompanying Kathleen. It was her husband. The beard was unfamiliar, but I recognised beneath it his enormous mouth, the bright sensuous lips, the large brown eyes forever brimming with pathos.

It was not for me to speak to Kathleen, but I had a sudden inspiration which caused me to say quietly,

'Hallo, George.'

The giant of a man turned round to face the direction of my voice. There were so many people — but at length he saw me.

'Hallo, George,' I said again.

Kathleen had started to haggle with the stall-owner, in her old way, over the price of the jade ring. George continued to stare at me, his big mouth slightly parted so that I could see a wide slit of red lips and white

teeth between the fair grassy growths of beard and
moustache.

'My God!' he said.

'What's the matter?' said Kathleen.

'Hallo, George!' I said again, quite loud this time,
and cheerfully.

'Look!' said George. 'Look who's there, over beside
the fruit stall.'

Kathleen looked but didn't see.

'Who is it?' she said impatiently.

'It's Needle,' he said. 'She said "Hallo, George".'

'*Needle*,' said Kathleen. 'Who do you mean. You
don't mean our old friend *Needle* who——'

'Yes. There she is. My God!'

He looked very ill, although when I had said 'Hallo,
George' I had spoken friendly enough.

'I don't see anyone faintly resembling poor Needle,'
said Kathleen looking at him. She was worried.

George pointed straight at me. 'Look *there*. I tell
you that is Needle.'

'You're ill, George. Heavens, you must be seeing
things. Come on home. Needle isn't there. You know
as well as I do, Needle is dead.'

I must explain that I departed this life nearly five
years ago. But I did not altogether depart this world.
There were those odd things still to be done which
one's executors can never do properly. Papers to be
looked over, even after the executors have torn them
up. Lots of business except, of course, on Sundays
and Holidays of Obligation, plenty to take an interest
in for the time being. I take my recreation on Saturday
mornings. If it is a wet Saturday I wander up and

down the substantial lanes of Woolworth's as I did when
I was young and visible. There is a pleasurable spread
of objects on the counters which I now perceive and
exploit with a certain detachment, since it suits with
my condition of life. Creams, toothpastes, combs and
hankies, cotton gloves, flimsy flowering scarves, writing-
paper and crayons, ice-cream cones and orangeade,
screwdrivers, boxes of tacks, tins of paint, of glue, of
marmalade; I always liked them but far more now that
I have no need of any. When Saturdays are fine I go
instead to the Portobello Road where formerly I would
jaunt with Kathleen in our grown-up days. The
barrow-loads do not change much, of apples and rayon
vests in common blues and low-taste mauve, of silver
plate, trays and teapots long since changed hands from
the bygone citizens to dealers, from shops to the new
flats and breakable homes, and then over to the barrow-
stalls and the dealers again: Georgian spoons, rings,
ear-rings of turquoise and opal set in the butterfly
pattern of true-lovers' knot, patch-boxes with miniature
paintings of ladies on ivory, snuff-boxes of silver with
Scotch pebbles inset.

Sometimes as occasion arises on a Saturday morning,
my friend Kathleen, who is a Catholic, has a Mass said
for my soul, and then I am in attendance as it were at
the church. But most Saturdays I take my delight
among the solemn crowds with their aimless purposes,
their eternal life not far away, who push past the
counters and stalls, who handle, buy, steal, touch,
desire and ogle the merchandise. I hear the tinkling
tills, I hear the jangle of loose change and tongues and
children wanting to hold and have.

That is how I came to be in the Portobello Road that

Saturday morning when I saw George and Kathleen. I would not have spoken had I not been inspired to it. Indeed it's one of the things I can't do now — to speak out, unless inspired. And most extraordinary, on that morning as I spoke, a degree of visibility set in. I suppose from poor George's point of view it was like seeing a ghost when he saw me standing by the fruit barrow repeating in so friendly a manner, 'Hallo, George!'

We were bound for the south. When our education, what we could get of it from the north, was thought to be finished, one by one we were sent or sent for to London. John Skinner whom we called Skinny went to study more archæology, George to join his uncle's tobacco farm, Kathleen to stay with her rich connections and to potter intermittently in the Mayfair hat shop which one of them owned. A little later I also went to London to see life, for it was my ambition to write about life, which first I had to see.

'We four must stick together,' George said very often in that yearning way of his. He was always desperately afraid of neglect. We four looked likely to shift off in different directions and George did not trust the other three of us not to forget all about him. More and more as the time came for him to depart for his uncle's tobacco farm in Africa he said,

'We four must keep in touch.'

And before he left he told each of us anxiously,

'I'll write regularly, once a month. We must keep together for the sake of the old times.' He had three prints taken from the negative of that photo on the haystack, wrote on the back of them, 'George took this

the day that Needle found the needle' and gave us a
copy each. I think we all wished he could become a bit
more callous.

During my lifetime I was a drifter, nothing organised.
It was difficult for my friends to follow the logic of my
life. By the normal reckonings I should have come to
starvation and ruin, which I never did. Of course, I did
not live to write about life as I wanted to do. Possibly
that is why I am inspired to do so now in these peculiar
circumstances.

I taught in a private school in Kensington for almost
three months, very small children. I didn't know
what to do with them but I was kept fairly busy escort-
ing incontinent little boys to the lavatory and telling
the little girls to use their handkerchiefs. After that I
lived a winter holiday in London on my small capital,
and when that had run out I found a diamond bracelet
in the cinema for which I received a reward of fifty
pounds. When it was used up I got a job with a
publicity man, writing speeches for absorbed in-
dustrialists, in which the dictionary of quotations
came in very useful. So it went on. I got engaged to
Skinny, but shortly after that I was left a small legacy,
enough to keep me for six months. This somehow
decided me that I didn't love Skinny so I gave him
back the ring.

But it was through Skinny that I went to Africa.
He was engaged with a party of researchers to investi-
gate King Solomon's mines, that series of ancient
workings ranging from the ancient port of Ophir, now
called Beira, across Portuguese East Africa and Southern
Rhodesia to the mighty jungle-city of Zimbabwe whose
temple walls still stand by the approach to an ancient

and sacred mountain, where the rubble of that civili-
sation scatters itself over the surrounding Rhodesian
waste. I accompanied the party as a sort of secretary.
Skinny vouched for me, he paid my fare, he sympathised
by his action with my inconsequential life although
when he spoke of it he disapproved. A life like mine
annoys most people; they go to their jobs every day,
attend to things, give orders, pummel typewriters, and
get two or three weeks off every year, and it vexes them
to see someone else not bothering to do these things
and yet getting away with it, not starving, being lucky
as they call it. Skinny, when I had broken off our
engagement, lectured me about this, but still he took
me to Africa knowing I should probably leave his
unit within a few months.

We were there a few weeks before we began enquiring for George who was farming about four hundred
miles away to the north. We had not told him of our
plans.

'If we tell George to expect us in his part of the
world he'll come rushing to pester us the first week.
After all, we're going on business,' Skinny had said.

Before we left Kathleen told us, 'Give George my
love and tell him not to send frantic cables every time
I don't answer his letters right away. Tell him I'm
busy in the hat shop and being presented. You would
think he hadn't another friend in the world the way he
carries on.'

We had settled first at Fort Victoria, our nearest
place of access to the Zimbabwe ruins. There we made
enquiries about George. It was clear he hadn't many
friends. The older settlers were the most tolerant
about the half-caste woman he was living with, as we

found, but they were furious about his methods of raising tobacco which we learned were most unprofessional and in some mysterious way disloyal to the whites. We could never discover how it was that George's style of tobacco farming gave the blacks opinions about themselves, but that's what the older settlers claimed. The newer immigrants thought he was unsociable and, of course, his living with that nig made visiting impossible.

I must say I was myself a bit off-put by this news about the brown woman. I was brought up in a university town to which came Indian, African and Asiatic students in a variety of tints and hues. I was brought up to avoid them for reasons connected with local reputation and God's ordinances. You cannot easily go against what you were brought up to do unless you are a rebel by nature.

Anyhow, we visited George eventually, taking advantage of the offer of transport from some people bound north in search of game. He had heard of our arrival in Rhodesia and though he was glad, almost relieved, to see us he pursued a policy of sullenness for the first hour.

'We wanted to give you a surprise, George.'

'How were we to know that you'd get to hear of our arrival, George? News here must travel faster than light, George.'

'We did hope to give you a surprise, George.'

We flattered and 'Georged' him until at last he said, 'Well, I must say it's good to see you. All we need now is Kathleen. We four simply must stick together. You find when you're in a place like this, there's nothing like old friends.'

He showed us his drying sheds. He showed us a paddock where he was experimenting with a horse and a zebra mare, attempting to mate them. They were frolicking happily, but not together. They passed each other in their private play time and again, but without acknowledgment and without resentment.

'It's been done before,' George said. 'It makes a fine strong beast, more intelligent than a mule and sturdier than a horse. But I'm not having any success with this pair, they won't look at each other.'

After a while, he said, "Come in for a drink and meet Matilda.'

She was dark brown, with a subservient hollow chest and round shoulders, a gawky woman, very snappy with the houseboys. We said pleasant things as we drank on the stoep before dinner, but we found George difficult. For some reason he began to rail at me for breaking off my engagement to Skinny, saying what a dirty trick it was after all those good times in the old days. I diverted attention to Matilda. I supposed, I said, she knew this part of the country well?

'No,' said she, 'I been a-shellitered my life. I not put out to working. Me nothing to go from place to place is allowed like dirty girls does.' In her speech she gave every syllable equal stress.

George explained, 'Her father was a white magistrate in Natal. She had a sheltered upbringing, different from the other coloureds, you realise.'

'Man, me no black-eyed Susan,' said Matilda, 'no, no.'

On the whole, George treated her as a servant. She was about four months advanced in pregnancy, but he made her get up and fetch for him, many times.

Soap: that was one of the things Matilda had to fetch. George made his own bath soap, showed it proudly, gave us the receipt which I did not trouble to remember; I was fond of nice soaps during my lifetime and George's smelt of brilliantine and looked likely to soil one's skin.

'D'yo brahn?' Matilda asked me.

George said, 'She is asking if you go brown in the sun.'

'No, I go freckled.'

'I got sister-in-law go freckles.'

She never spoke another word to Skinny nor to me, and we never saw her again.

Some months later I said to Skinny,

'I'm fed up with being a camp-follower.'

He was not surprised that I was leaving his unit, but he hated my way of expressing it. He gave me a Presbyterian look.

'Don't talk like that. Are you going back to England or staying?'

'Staying, for a while.'

'Well, don't wander too far off.'

I was able to live on the fee I got for writing a gossip column in a local weekly, which wasn't my idea of writing about life, of course. I made friends, more than I could cope with, after I left Skinny's exclusive little band of archaeologists. I had the attractions of being newly out from England and of wanting to see life. Of the countless young men and go-ahead families who purred me along the Rhodesian roads, hundred after hundred miles, I only kept up with one family when I returned to my native land. I think that was because they were the most representative, they stood for all the rest: people in those parts are very typical of each other, as one group of standing stones in that wilderness is like the next.

I met George once more in a hotel in Bulawayo. We drank highballs and spoke of war. Skinny's party were just then deciding whether to remain in the country or return home. They had reached an exciting part of their research, and whenever I got a chance to visit Zimbabwe he would take me for a moonlight walk in the ruined temple and try to make me see phantom Phœnicians flitting ahead of us, or along the walls. I had half a mind to marry Skinny; perhaps, I thought, when his studies were finished. The impending war was in our bones: so I remarked to George as we sat drinking highballs on the hotel stoep in the hard bright sunny July winter of that year.

George was inquisitive about my relations with Skinny. He tried to pump me for about half an hour and when at last I said, 'You are becoming aggressive, George,' he stopped. He became quite pathetic. He said, 'War or no war I'm clearing out of this.'

'It's the heat does it,' I said.

'I'm clearing out in any case. I've lost a fortune in tobacco. My uncle is making a fuss. It's the other bloody planters; once you get the wrong side of them you're finished in this wide land.'

'What about Matilda?' I asked.

He said, 'She'll be all right. She's got hundreds of relatives.'

I had already heard about the baby girl. Coal black, by repute, with George's features. And another on the way, they said.

'What about the child?'

He didn't say anything to that. He ordered more highballs and when they arrived he swizzled his for a long time with a stick. 'Why didn't you ask me to your twenty-first?' he said then.

'I didn't have anything special, no party, George. We had a quiet drink among ourselves, George, just Skinny and the old professors ánd two of the wives and me, George.'

'You didn't ask me to your twenty-first,' he said. 'Kathleen writes to me regularly.'

This wasn't true. Kathleen sent me letters fairly often in which she said, 'Don't tell George I wrote to you as he will be expecting word from me and I can't be bothered actually.'

'But you,' said George, 'don't seem to have any sense of old friendships, you and Skinny.'

'Oh, George!' I said.

'Remember the times we had,' George said. 'We used to have times.' His large brown eyes began to water.

'I'll have to be getting along,' I said.

'Please don't go. Don't leave me just yet. I've something to tell you.'

'Something nice?' I laid on an eager smile. All responses to George had to be overdone.

'You don't know how lucky you are,' George said.

'How?' I said. Sometimes I got tired of being called lucky by everybody. There were times when, privately practising my writings about life, I knew the bitter side of my fortune. When I failed again and again to reproduce life in some satisfactory and perfect form,

I was the more imprisoned, for all my carefree living, within my craving for this satisfaction. Sometimes, in my impotence and need I secreted a venom which infected all my life for days on end and which spurted out indiscriminately on Skinny or on anyone who crossed my path.

'You aren't bound by anyone,' George said. 'You come and go as you please. Something always turns up for you. You're free, and you don't know your luck.'

'You're a damn sight more free than I am,' I said sharply. 'You've got your rich uncle.'

'He's losing interest in me,' George said. 'He's had enough.'

'Oh well, you're young yet. What was it you wanted to tell me?'

'A secret,' George said. 'Remember we used to have those secrets.'

'Oh, yes we did.'

'Did you ever tell any of mine?'

'Oh no, George.' In reality, I couldn't remember any particular secret out of the dozens we must have exchanged from our schooldays onwards.

'Well, this is a secret, mind. Promise not to tell.'

'Promise.'

'I'm married.'

'Married, George! Oh, who to?'

'Matilda.'

'How dreadful!' I spoke before I could think, but he agreed with me.

'Yes, it's awful, but what could I do?'

'You might have asked my advice,' I said pompously.

'I'm two years older than you are. I don't ask advice from you, Needle, little beast.'

'Don't ask for sympathy then.'

'A nice friend you are,' he said, 'I must say after all these years.'

'Poor George!' I said.

'There are three white men to one white woman in this country,' said George. 'An isolated planter doesn't see a white woman and if he sees one she doesn't see him. What could I do? I needed the woman.'

I was nearly sick. One, because of my Scottish upbringing. Two, because of my horror of corny phrases like 'I needed the woman', which George repeated twice again.

'And Matilda got tough,' said George, 'after you and Skinny came to visit us. She had some friends at the Mission, and she packed up and went to them.'

'You should have let her go,' I said.

'I went after her,' George said. 'She insisted on being married, so I married her.'

'That's not a proper secret, then,' I said. 'The news of a mixed marriage soon gets about.'

'I took care of that,' George said. 'Crazy as I was, I took her to the Congo and married her there. She promised to keep quiet about it.'

'Well, you can't clear off and leave her now, surely,' I said.

'I'm going to get out of this place. I can't stand the woman and I can't stand the country. I didn't realise what it would be like. Two years of the country and three months of my wife has been enough.'

'Will you get a divorce?'

'No, Matilda's Catholic. She won't divorce.'

George was fairly getting through the highballs, and I wasn't far behind him. His brown eyes floated shiny and liquid as he told me how he had written to tell his uncle of his plight, 'Except, of course, I didn't say we were married, that would have been too much for him. He's a prejudiced hardened old Colonial. I only said I'd had a child by a coloured woman and was expecting another, and he perfectly understood. He came at once by plane a few weeks ago. He's made a settlement on her, providing she keeps her mouth shut about her association with me.'

'Will she do that?'

'Oh, yes, or she won't get the money.'

'But as your wife she has a claim on you, in any case.'

'If she claimed as my wife she'd get far less. Matilda know what she's doing, greedy bitch she is. She'll keep her mouth shut.'

'Only, you won't be able to marry again, will you, George?'

'Not unless she dies,' he said. 'And she's as strong as a trek ox.'

'Well, I'm sorry, George,' I said.

'Good of you to say so,' he said. 'But I can see by your chin that you disapprove of me. Even my old uncle understood.'

'Oh, George, I quite understand. You were lonely, I suppose.'

'You didn't even ask me to your twenty-first. If you and Skinny had been nicer to me, I would never have lost my head and married the woman, never.'

'You didn't ask me to your wedding,' I said.

'You're a catty bissom, Needle, not like what you

were in the old times when you used to tell us your
wee stories.'

'I'll have to be getting along,' I said.

'Mind you keep the secret,' George said.

'Can't I tell Skinny? He would be very sorry for
you, George.'

'You mustn't tell anyone. Keep it a secret. Promise.'

'Promise,' I said. I understood that he wished to
enforce some sort of bond between us with this secret,
and I thought, 'Oh well, I suppose he's lonely. Keeping his secret won't do any harm.'

I returned to England with Skinny's party just before
the war.

I did not see George again till just before my death,
five years ago.

After the war Skinny returned to his studies. He
had two more exams, over a period of eighteen months,
and I thought I might marry him when the exams
were over.

'You might do worse than Skinny,' Kathleen used
to say to me on our Saturday morning excursions to
the antique shops and the junk stalls.

She too was getting on in years. The remainder of
our families in Scotland were hinting that it was time
we settled down with husbands. Kathleen was a little
younger than me, but looked much older. She knew
her chances were diminishing but at that time I did not
think she cared very much. As for myself, the main
attraction of marrying Skinny was his prospective
expeditions to Mesopotamia. My desire to marry him
had to be stimulated by the continual reading of books
about Babylon and Assyria; perhaps Skinny felt this,

because he supplied the books and even started instructing me in the art of deciphering cuneiform tables.

Kathleen was more interested in marriage than I thought. Like me, she had racketed around a good deal during the war; she had actually been engaged to an officer in the U.S. navy, who was killed. Now she kept an antique shop near Lambeth, was doing very nicely, lived in a Chelsea square, but for all that she must have wanted to be married and have children. She would stop and look into all the prams which the mothers had left outside shops or area gates.

'The poet Swinburne used to do that,' I told her once.

'Really? Did he want children of his own?'

'I shouldn't think so. He simply liked babies.'

Before Skinny's final exam he fell ill and was sent to a sanatorium in Switzerland.

'You're fortunate after all not to be married to him,' Kathleen said. 'You might have caught T.B.'

I was fortunate, I was lucky . . . so everyone kept telling me on different occasions. Although it annoyed me to hear, I knew they were right, but in a way that was different from what they meant. It took me very small effort to make a living; book reviews, odd jobs for Kathleen, a few months with the publicity man again, still getting up speeches about literature, art and life for industrial tycoons. I was waiting to write about life and it seemed to me that the good fortune lay in this, whenever it should be. And until then I was assured of my charmed life, the necessities of existence always coming my way and I with far more leisure than anyone else. I thought of my type of luck after I became a Catholic and was being confirmed. The Bishop touches

the candidate on the cheek, a symbolic reminder of the
sufferings a Christian is supposed to undertake. I
thought, how lucky, what a feathery symbol to stand
for the hellish violence of its true meaning.

I visited Skinny twice in the two years that he was in
the sanatorium. He was almost cured, and expected to
be home within a few months. I told Kathleen after my
last visit.

'Maybe I'll marry Skinny when he's well again.'

'Make it definite, Needle, and not so much of the
maybe. You don't know when you're well off,' she
said.

This was five years ago, in the last year of my life.
Kathleen and I had become very close friends. We
met several times each week, and after our Saturday
morning excursions in the Portobello Road very often
I would accompany Kathleen to her aunt's house in
Kent for a long week-end.

One day in the June of that year I met Kathleen
specially for lunch because she had phoned me to say
she had news.

'Guess who came into the shop this afternoon,' she
said.

'Who?'

'George.'

We had half imagined George was dead. We had
received no letters in the past ten years. Early in the
war we had heard rumours of his keeping a night club
in Durban, but nothing after that. We could have
made enquiries if we had felt moved to do so.

At one time, when we discussed him, Kathleen had
said,

'I ought to get in touch with poor George. But then

I think he would write back. He would demand a regular correspondence again.'

'We four must stick together,' I mimicked.

'I can visualise his reproachful limpid orbs,' Kathleen said.

Skinny said, 'He's probably gone native. With his coffee concubine and a dozen mahogany kids.'

'Perhaps he's dead,' Kathleen said.

I did not speak of George's marriage, nor of any of his confidences in the hotel at Bulawayo. As the years passed we ceased to mention him except in passing, as someone more or less dead so far as we were concerned.

Kathleen was excited about George's turning up. She had forgotten her impatience with him in former days; she said,

'It was so wonderful to see old George. He seems to need a friend, feels neglected, out of touch with things.'

'He needs mothering, I suppose.'

Kathleen didn't notice the malice. She declared, 'That's exactly the case with George. It always has been, I can see it now.'

She seemed ready to come to any rapid new and happy conclusion about George. In the course of the morning he had told her of his wartime night club in Durban, his game-shooting expeditions since. It was clear he had not mentioned Matilda. He had put on weight, Kathleen told me, but he could carry it.

I was curious to see this version of George, but I was leaving for Scotland next day and did not see him till September of that year just before my death.

While I was in Scotland I gathered from Kathleen's letters that she was seeing George very frequently, finding enjoyable company in him, looking after him. 'You'll be surprised to see how he has developed.' Apparently he would hang round Kathleen in her shop most days, 'it makes him feel useful' as she maternally expressed it. He had an old relative in Kent whom he visited at weekends; this old lady lived a few miles from Kathleen's aunt, which made it easy for them to travel down together on Saturdays, and go for long country walks.

'You'll see such a difference in George,' Kathleen said on my return to London in September. I was to meet him that night, a Saturday. Kathleen's aunt was abroad, the maid on holiday, and I was to keep Kathleen company in the empty house.

George had left London for Kent a few days earlier. 'He's actually helping with the harvest down there!' Kathleen told me lovingly.

Kathleen and I planned to travel down together, but on that Saturday she was unexpectedly delayed in London on some business. It was arranged that I should go ahead of her in the early afternoon to see to the provisions for our party; Kathleen had invited George to dinner at her aunt's house that night.

'I should be with you by seven,' she said. 'Sure you won't mind the empty house? I hate arriving at empty houses, myself.'

I said no, I liked an empty house.

So I did, when I got there. I had never found the house more likeable. A large Georgian vicarage in about eight acres, most of the rooms shut and sheeted, there being only one servant. I discovered that I wouldn't need to go shopping, Kathleen's aunt had left many and delicate supplies with notes attached to them: 'Eat this up please do, see also fridge' and 'A treat for three hungry people see also 2 bttles beaune for yr party on back kn table.' It was like a treasure hunt as I followed clue after clue through the cool silent domestic quarters. A house in which there are no people — but with all the signs of tenancy — can be a most tranquil good place. People take up space in a house out of proportion to their size. On my previous visits I had seen the rooms overflowing as it seemed, with Kathleen, her aunt, and the little fat maidservant; they were always on the move. As I wandered through that part of the house which was in use, opening windows to let in the pale yellow air of September, I was not conscious that I, Needle, was taking up any space at all, I might have been a ghost.

The only thing to be fetched was the milk. I waited till after four when the milking should be done, then set off for the farm which lay across two fields at the back of the orchard. There, when the byreman was handing me the bottle, I saw George.

'Hallo, George,' I said.

'Needle! What are you doing here?' he said.

'Fetching milk,' I said.

'So am I. Well, it's good to see you, I must say.'

As we paid the farm-hand, George said, 'I'll walk back with you part of the way. But I mustn't stop, my old cousin's without any milk for her tea. How's Kathleen?'

'She was kept in London. She's coming on later, about seven, she expects.'

We had reached the end of the first field. George's way led to the left and on to the main road.

'We'll see you tonight, then?' I said.

'Yes, and talk about old times.'

'Grand,' I said.

But George got over the stile with me.

'Look here,' he said. 'I'd like to talk to you, Needle.'

'We'll talk tonight, George. Better not keep your cousin waiting for the milk.' I found myself speaking to him almost as if he were a child.

'No, I want to talk to you alone. This is a good opportunity.'

We began to cross the second field. I had been hoping to have the house to myself for a couple more hours and I was rather petulant.

'See,' he said suddenly, 'that haystack.'

'Yes,' I said absently.

'Let's sit there and talk. I'd like to see you up on a haystack again. I still keep that photo. Remember that time when——'

'I found the needle,' I said very quickly, to get it over.

But I was glad to rest. The stack had been broken up, but we managed to find a nest in it. I buried my bottle of milk in the hay for coolness. George placed his carefully at the foot of the stack.

'My old cousin is terribly vague, poor soul. A bit hazy in her head. She hasn't the least sense of time. If I tell her I've only been gone ten minutes she'll believe it.'

I giggled, and looked at him. His face had grown much larger, his lips full, wide and with a ripe colour that is strange in a man. His brown eyes were abounding as before with some inarticulate plea.

'So you're going to marry Skinny after all these years?'

'I really don't know, George.'

'You played him up properly.'

'It isn't for you to judge. I have my own reasons for what I do.'

'Don't get sharp,' he said, 'I was only funning.' To prove it, he lifted a tuft of hay and brushed my face with it.

'D'you know,' he said next, 'I didn't think you and Skinny treated me very decently in Rhodesia.'

'Well, we were busy, George. And we were younger then, we had a lot to do and see. After all, we could see you any other time, George.'

'A touch of selfishness,' he said.

'I'll have to be getting along, George.' I made to get down from the stack.

He pulled me back. 'Wait, I've got something to tell you.'

'O.K., George, tell me.'

'First promise not to tell Kathleen. She wants it kept a secret so that she can tell you herself.'

'All right. Promise.'

'I'm going to marry Kathleen.'

'But you're already married.'

Sometimes I heard news of Matilda from the one Rhodesian family with whom I still kept up. They referred to her as 'George's Dark Lady' and of course they did not know he was married to her. She had apparently made a good thing out of George, they said, for she minced around all tarted up, never did a stroke of work and was always unsettling the respectable coloured girls in their neighbourhood. According to accounts, she was a living example of the folly of behaving as George did.

'I married Matilda in the Congo,' George was saying.

'It would still be bigamy,' I said.

He was furious when I used that word bigamy. He lifted a handful of hay as if he would throw it in my face, but controlling himself meanwhile he fanned it at me playfully.

'I'm not sure that the Congo marriage was valid,' he continued. 'Anyway, as far as I'm concerned, it isn't.'

'You can't do a thing like that,' I said.

'I need Kathleen. She's been decent to me. I think we were always meant for each other, me and Kathleen.'

'I'll have to be going,' I said.

But he put his knee over my ankles, so that I couldn't move. I sat still and gazed into space.

He tickled my face with a wisp of hay.

'Smile up, Needle,' he said; 'let's talk like old times.'

'Well?'

'No one knows about my marriage to Matilda except you and me.'

'And Matilda,' I said.

'She'll hold her tongue so long as she gets her payments. My uncle left an annuity for the purpose, his lawyers see to it.'

'Let me go, George.'

'You promised to keep it a secret,' he said, 'you promised.'

'Yes, I promised.'

'And now that you're going to marry Skinny, we'll be properly coupled off as we should have been years ago. We should have been — but youth! — our youth got in the way, didn't it?'

209

'Life got in the way,' I said.

'But everything's going to be all right now. You'll keep my secret, won't you? You promised.' He had released my feet. I edged a little further from him.

I said, 'If Kathleen intends to marry you, I shall tell her that you're already married.'

'You wouldn't do a dirty trick like that, Needle? You're going to be happy with Skinny, you wouldn't stand in the way of my——'

'I must, Kathleen's my best friend,' I said swiftly.

He looked as if he would murder me and he did, he stuffed hay into my mouth until it could hold no more, kneeling on my body to keep it still, holding both my wrists tight in his huge left hand. I saw the red full lines of his mouth and the white slit of his teeth last thing on earth. Not another soul passed by as he pressed my body into the stack, as he made a deep nest for me, tearing up the hay to make a groove the length of my corpse, and finally pulling the warm dry stuff in a mound over this concealment, so natural-looking in a broken haystack. Then George climbed down, took up his bottle of milk and went his way. I suppose that was why he looked so unwell when I stood, nearly five years later, by the barrow in the Portobello Road and said in easy tones, 'Hallo, George!'

The Haystack Murder was one of the notorious crimes of that year.

My friends said, 'A girl who had everything to live for.'

After a search that lasted twenty hours, when my body was found, the evening papers said, '"Needle" is found: in haystack!'

Kathleen, speaking from that Catholic point of view which takes some getting used to, said, 'She was at Confession only the day before she died — wasn't she lucky?'

The poor byre-hand who sold us the milk was grilled for hour after hour by the local police, and later by Scotland Yard. So was George. He admitted walking as far as the haystack with me, but he denied lingering there.

'You hadn't seen your friend for ten years?' the Inspector asked him.

'That's right,' said George.

'And you didn't stop to have a chat?'

'No. We'd arranged to meet later at dinner. My cousin was waiting for the milk, I couldn't stop.'

The old soul, his cousin, swore that he hadn't been gone more than ten minutes in all, and she believed it to the day of her death a few months later. There was the microscopic evidence of hay on George's jacket, of course, but the same evidence was on every man's jacket in the district that fine harvest year. Unfortunately, the byreman's hands were even brawnier and mightier than George's. The marks on my wrists had been done by such hands, so the laboratory charts indicated when my post-mortem was all completed. But the wrist-marks weren't enough to pin down the crime to either man. If I hadn't been wearing my long-sleeved cardigan, it was said, the bruises might have matched up properly with someone's fingers.

Kathleen, to prove that George had absolutely no motive, told the police that she was engaged to him. George thought this a little foolish. They checked up on his life in Africa, right back to his living with

Matilda. But the marriage didn't come out — who would think of looking up registers in the Congo? Not that this would have proved any motive for murder. All the same, George was relieved when the enquiries were over without the marriage to Matilda being disclosed. He was able to have his nervous breakdown at the same time as Kathleen had hers, and they recovered together and got married, long after the police had shifted their enquiries to an Air Force camp five miles from Kathleen's aunt's home. Only a lot of excitement and drinks came of those investigations. The Haystack Murder was one of the unsolved crimes that year.

Shortly afterwards the byre-hand emigrated to Canada to start afresh, with the help of Skinny who felt sorry for him.

After seeing George taken away home by Kathleen that Saturday in the Portobello Road, I thought that perhaps I might be seeing more of him in similar circumstances. The next Saturday I looked out for him, and at last there he was, without Kathleen, half-worried, half-hopeful.

I dashed his hopes. I said, 'Hallo, George!'

He looked in my direction, rooted in the midst of the flowing market-mongers in that convivial street. I thought to myself, 'He looks as if he had a mouthful of hay.' It was the new bristly maize-coloured beard and moustache surrounding his great mouth suggested the thought, gay and lyrical as life.

'Hallo, George!' I said again.

I might have been inspired to say more on that agreeable morning, but he didn't wait. He was away down a side street and along another street and down one more, zig-zag, as far and as devious as he could take himself from the Portobello Road.

Nevertheless he was back again next week. Poor Kathleen had brought him in her car. She left it at the top of the street, and got out with him, holding him tight by the arm. It grieved me to see Kathleen ignoring the spread of scintillations on the stalls. I had myself seen a charming Battersea box quite to her taste, also a pair of enamelled silver earrings. But she took no notice of these wares, clinging close to George, and, poor Kathleen — I hate to say how she looked.

And George was haggard. His eyes seemed to have got smaller as if he had been recently in pain. He advanced up the road with Kathleen on his arm, letting himself lurch from side to side with his wife bobbing beside him, as the crowds asserted their rights of way.

'Oh, George!' I said. 'You don't look at all well, George.'

'Look!' said George. 'Over there by the hardware barrow. That's Needle.'

Kathleen was crying. 'Come back home, dear,' she said.

'Oh, you don't look well, George!' I said.

They took him to a nursing home. He was fairly quiet, except on Saturday mornings when they had a hard time of it to keep him indoors and away from the Portobello Road.

But a couple of months later he did escape. It was a Monday.

They searched for him in the Portobello Road, but actually he had gone off to Kent to the village near the scene of the Haystack Murder. There he went to the police and gave himself up, but they could tell from the way he was talking that there was something wrong with the man.

'I saw Needle in the Portobello Road three Saturdays running,' he explained, 'and they put me in a private ward but I got away while the nurses were seeing to the new patient. You remember the murder of Needle — well, I did it. Now you know the truth, and that will keep bloody Needle's mouth shut.'

Dozens of poor mad fellows confess to every murder. The police obtained an ambulance to take him back to the nursing home. He wasn't there long. Kathleen gave up her shop and devoted herself to looking after him at home. But she found that the Saturday mornings were a strain. He insisted on going to see me in the Portobello Road and would come back to insist that he'd murdered Needle. Once he tried to tell her something about Matilda, but Kathleen was so kind and solicitous, I don't think he had the courage to remember what he had to say.

Skinny had always been rather reserved with George since the murder. But he was kind to Kathleen. It was he who persuaded them to emigrate to Canada so that George should be well out of reach of the Portobello Road.

George has recovered somewhat in Canada but of course he will never be the old George again, as Kathleen writes to Skinny. 'That Haystack tragedy did for George,' she writes. 'I feel sorrier for George sometimes than I am for poor Needle. But I do often have Masses said for Needle's soul.'

I doubt if George will ever see me again in the Portobello Road. He broods much over the crumpled